Unwanted Love

Unwanted Series

Brooke Olivia

Playlist

Luc & Ambre

"**Ribs**"- *Lorde*

"**Us**" - *James Bay*

"**Take on the world**" - *You and me at six*

"**Love me or leave me**" - *Little mix*

"**Always been you**" - *Jessie Murph*

"**Piece by piece**" - *Kelly Clarkson*

"**I should have kissed you**" - *One direction*

"**Paris**"- *Sabrina Carpenter*

"**Still into you**" - *Paramore*

"**You are in love**" - *Taylor Swift*

"**Dress**" - *Taylor Swift*

"**Can I be him**" - *James Arthur*

"**Memories**" - *Conan Gray*

"**Crush**" - *David Archuleta*

"**That way**" - *Tate McRae*

For the people who find comfort in the pages of a book, welcome home...

Prologue

Ten years earlier

Luc

"Mama, what time will you be home?"

I miss my Mama. She's been away on work trips for weeks, now she's on a ferry ride home in a storm. Which terrifies me. It can't be safe to be on the sea in a storm, right? Mama told me all will be okay, though, and she's safe. I've been at home alone with Eric and my baby brother. Eric is my Mama's husband. They got married about several years before Henry was born when I was about three! Henry is one now! I'll be honest, I don't really like Eric, I know that's mean, but he's nice to my brother but terrible to me. I don't understand, and I wish he could see me as a son. It's hard not having a Papa.

"I'll be home in about three hours, baby. The ferry is due to arrive shortly. Okay?"

That relieves me. She will be home soon. I can tell her how much I've missed her. Of course, I should also tell her what Eric said to me. The last thing I want is to upset my Mama or give Eric more reason to yell at me. He can be very frightening, and even dangerous. Only around me, though. I'm safe with my Mama. Eric doesn't show this side of him around Mama.

She carries on. "If you need anything, just ask Eric, okay. He's always there as well as me, you can talk to him." But I can't. That's what I want to tell her. *If only she knew.* If only she knew the man he is when she's not around. But I keep quiet. It's easier that way.

"Okay, Mama, I love you."

"I love you too, my baby boy."

I could really do with a hug from her right now. My Mama has always been my best friend. She's always there to play games with me, or draw with me, she even takes time away from work to spend more time with me, she's the perfect Mama. Then there's Ambre, of course. Maybe I should call Ambre and see if she wants to come round to my house. Ambre always cheers me up.

I begin dialling her number. She hasn't been to my house since my Mama has been away. I sense that she feels as uneasy around Eric as I do. Suddenly my phone is grabbed harshly from my hand.

"Lucas, what do you think you're doing? Calling that *brat* without my permission, in *my* house." He spits out. "You go by my rules when I'm in charge. Why do you even have a phone? You're seven!"

"I'd rather be called Luc. You know this. And my Ambre is not in any way a brat." I say, looking down to the floor.

"I'll call you whatever the hell I want! And a little piece of fatherly advice, stop calling her yours. It's never going to happen. She'll leave you just like everyone else." He spits with a sly smile. I'm tired of hearing him shouting. I don't even feel safe around Eric. So I run to my room holding back the tears until I'm out of his sight. Maybe if I stay here until my Mama gets home, I'll be safe. Eric doesn't shout when Mama is home. I wish she was always home.

I'm sure only hours have passed but it feels like days. Then, I hear heavy footsteps pounding up the stairs. I'm *sure* I haven't done anything; I haven't even moved from my bed since I got here. I silently pray he's not mad because I'm the one who will get the wrath.

The door barges open, but the look on his face doesn't look like anger, not *just* anger anyway. He looks *sad*. And he's holding the phone to me? Why? Cautiously I take the phone from his hand, seeing he's talking to my Mama. I put the phone up to my ear, completely confused.

"Hey, Mama! Are you nearly home yet? I miss you so much and as soon as you get home, I'm gonna smother you with cuddles so you can never leave me again!" I say, giggling. Just speaking to my Mama makes me that little bit happier. But when Eric glares at me darkly, my smile fades.

"Hey, baby! I miss you so much. You don't understand how much my boy." She's crying. Why is she crying? She should be happy. She's home soon. She gets to see me after so long. I don't understand.

"I'm not going to be home like I planned, baby. I'm so sorry. I'm going to take another adventure. A really long one this time, though. You won't see me for a long, long time, okay?"

What? What does she mean? She can't leave me again.

I need her. I can't stay here with Eric. I don't think I'll survive.

"I don't understand, Mama. Where are you going? Please, come home. I need you home with me. What about Henry? Me and Henry need you more than your job!" My voice breaks and tears start falling from my eyes uncontrollably.

"I need you as well, my boy. Trust me, I do. I promise I would do anything to see you again one last time. It's going to be tough, but you can do it. You're just like your Papa. He was so strong, just like you."

She stops talking, and I hear her let out a cry far from the phone, clearly trying to hide it from me.

"I know you can get through this without me because you are a fighter! You have the biggest heart. And one day, you'll see me again. With your Papa as well! But that day is very far from today. For now, you will see me when you close your eyes, you will see me in your dreams, and at your toughest times, I will be standing right next to you. Smothering you with cuddles! You may not be able to see me, but I'll be there. I will always be there, especially when you're drawing. You'll never be drawing alone, baby. I promise."

She's leaving me. It hurts so much it feels like I can't breathe. Where has all the air gone? I feel broken. I feel like I'll never be happy again. Like I'll never smile again. What's the point of life without your favourite person?

Tears flow down my cheeks and onto my bed; I try to stop crying, it doesn't work. "I'm gonna miss you so much. Tell Papa I love him too, and I can't wait for the day I get to see him. Promise you will wait for me, Mama? You and Papa?" I can barely get a word out without having to stop and try to breathe. It hurts so much that my Mama is leaving me.

I will take care of my baby brother. And make sure he knows how much our Mama loves us. Just like my Mama did for me with my Papa. Henry will grow up knowing she was an angel. He'll know that everything we have now, we owe to her. She's our saviour.

"Of course, I promise. Papa and I will wait for you forever. But that day won't come for a *very* long time. So, for now, complete all your dreams, okay? Stay friends with Ambre forever. She's special. And know that if I could by some miracle change this, I would. I love you boys so much. Eric will take care of you for as long as you need him. You are in good hands, my boy. I love you. To the stars, an-" Her voice gets cut off by the sound of waves, screams, and beeping. What happened to you, Mama?

There was so much more I needed to say before Mama had to go on the new journey.

The water took my Mama. I will never get on a stupid boat, for as long as I live, I'm never going on the ocean.

I can't believe my Mama is gone. I can't smother her in cuddles as I planned to. I'm broken without her. I feel my body shaking, I can't stop. I don't know how to be rid of this pain. I don't understand how to go on from here.

I love you, Mama. To the stars and back. Then I hand Eric his phone and curl into my bed and let the tears fall, and fall and fall.

Ambre

My Mum just told me what happened to Luc's Mama. I really can't believe she's gone. It feels like my heart just cracked. I feel my hands tremble as I try to wrap my head around what I was just told. She was like a second Mum to me. Like my auntie. *She was family.* I can't even begin to imagine how my best friend must feel right now. He just lost his favourite person on this planet. His heart must be shattered.

I truly hope Eric is friendly to him; he is basically his Papa now. Even though nobody could ever replace his real Papa. At least his Mama and Papa have finally reunited again. Love reunited.

My Mum tells me that when people leave the world, they become angels. So that means his Mama is an angel now. She always has been such an angelic soul. And she can look after us all the time. I'll text Luc and tell him how his Mama can look after him as an angel. Maybe it'll make him feel better. I hope it does, anyway. Anything is worth a shot.

Ambre: Hi, my Luc. I miss you so much, it's unbelievable how much. my Mum just told me what's happened. I am so incredibly sorry about your Mama. I know my words won't mean much right now but I'm going to miss her so much. I'm sending all the hugs over the phone. And remember, she's an angel now, so she will always be by your side, making sure you don't do anything silly. I'll help with that too, of course. You will never be alone, mu Luc. I can promise you that.

Luc: Ambre, promise you'll never leave me? I don't know what I would do without you. I really do miss you. I could really do with one of your amazing hugs right now. I miss her so much already. I can't make my heart believe she's gone. My head knows she's not here anymore, but my heart is still holding onto hope that she'll walk through my door any second. The world is cruel. I can't believe they took my Mama from me.

Ambre: Luc, you don't even have to ask that. You know I'll never ever leave you. You will be my best friend forever and ever. I see the world is very mean, but we still have each other, so at least we have that. I will see you tomorrow for those hugs. My Mum and I are coming round to see you and baby Henry, get ready for a day of smiles, okay?

Luc: I'm looking forward. I don't feel like I'll ever smile again right now. I hope you can change that. Okay, see you tomorrow, Ambre. Thank you for messaging me. I know my Mama will always be with you as an angel as well; she has always loved you.

Ambre: I have always loved her too; she was like my second Mum. I love you lots, Luc. Forever and Always. You are my very best friend, don't forget that, okay?

Luc: I could never forget. I love you. Thank you, Ambre :)

I'm glad that he knows that he isn't alone. But I know Luc; it doesn't matter how many people tell him he is not alone, he will still feel alone. He told me that himself. Gosh, Luc, I'm sorry.

⚜ *Chapter 1* ⚜

Ambre

Today is going to be phenomenal. Today is the day Luc and I finally move into our apartment in *Paris*.

We decided on Paris when we were younger, it's always felt like that's where we're meant to be. My Mum used to live in Paris, as did Luc's, until they both moved here. They thought they'd honour France by giving their children French names, despite us living in London. Because of them, we know Paris is where we're meant to be. Neither of us is fluent in French, and we're only half French, from our Mums, but I know Paris will feel like home. We've been saving up for years to have enough. Now we're eighteen and going to this gorgeous university in Paris.

This has been a dream of ours since we were kids. To live together and go to the same university. Though we're not studying the same thing. I'm getting a degree in English literature.

Luc has yet to tell me what he's studying. It's a surprise. I'm not quite sure when or how he'll tell me. One of the many mysteries that is Luc.

But my dream, since I was a little girl, has always been to become an author. I write a little now and then, but I want to become a best-selling author. I want to write the most remarkable love story of all time. One that has everyone crying into their pillows because it's so heart-aching but also has them blushing at how adorable and loveable the characters are. Of course, I've got to add a bit of spice. And obviously, I must write a swoon-worthy morally grey book boyfriend for all the girls who find comfort in romance novels, like myself. I know it's going to take a while. But these things take time, and it's time I'm willing to take to make my dream come true. I need my readers to feel at home in these pages. This book has to be an escape for them. Somewhere they feel safe and understood. I want them to know that I see them, I feel with them, and this is all for them.

I'm all packed now, ready to get the plane to Paris. Ready to go *home*. The place I have always known is my home. The place I belong. I've packed my comfort reads, romance novels mainly. What can I say? I'm a hopeless romantic. Saying that I've never really had a real relationship, even though I've always craved that love. But I guess I just found that comfort in Luc instead. I think most boys feel threatened by Luc, how close we are, the fact he's literally my favourite person and nobody could take that place from him. I'm assuming no relationships will be happening this term because I'll be living with him. But who knows, maybe I'll meet someone who isn't so intimidated by Luc. Who understands. Unlikely, but hey! It doesn't bother me; I get more writing done alone, anyway. Luc is an exception; his words inspire me. When he's not being that annoying best friend. It's great having somebody there to read over my work and tell me what I could do differently though. I have a tendency to type too fast and put the letters in the wrong order. It drives me crazy. Luc notices. So having him there 24/7 might actually be good for me.

I say my goodbyes to my Mum and little sister. It's crazy weird to leave them, now it's just the two of them. Ami's Dad is off in LA, although he's still involved with her life, he's not present. And my Dad, well he was gone along time ago. I've never even met him. He took off before I could even open my eyes. Yeah, we don't like him.

Life's going to be so weird now, I've spent every evening with them watching movies for the entirety of my life. It's going to be different not being there. I hope I can cope with this difference. It'll be challenging, but I'll have Luc.

I hug my Mum goodbye and kiss my little sister on her head. The most upsetting part of all this is that I won't see Ami every day now. I can't be there after school to hear all about her gossip and all the school drama she loves telling me about. But, I'm sure she'll call me often. I hope she will. I promised to help her with her maths homework, despite also being hopeless when it comes to numeracy.

It's nearly time to board the plane. I'm so excited. Also nauseous. Very nauseous. I think it's the nerves of flying alone, and all this change.

"I'll miss you, my baby girl. I love you." My Mum says as she tears up. I hold back my own tears for her sake. If I start, we'll all be gone.

"Bye, Ambs! Have so much fun, don't stay in every night with Luc, like you do here. Go out! Obvs, don't be out drinking *all* night, but if you are, send me some pics, yeah? Love you!" I love my mini-me. I'll miss Ami more than anyone. She's always been my little best friend, Luc's as well. She's only fourteen but Ami's always been mature, like I have.

"Bye, Mum. I love you both so much. Ami, of course, I'll send you some pics at parties! Don't forget to call me with all your gossip and homework! Bye!"

"Everyone boarding the plane to Paris, please board now!" Then, finally, someone calls through the speakers; it's time to go.

I'm glad to finally be boarding, checking in my case was a rush, I swear I nearly missed the flight.

Boarding the plane alone feels like a breath of fresh air; I'm free to do whatever I want now. I'm free to go wherever, with whoever. But the only one I can think about is Luc. I'm going to be living the dream, literally living with my best friend. We can have endless movie nights and as many parties as we want. Movie nights will probably be a favourite. Movie nights with a hot chocolate in hand, rain pouring outside in the autumn breeze. Good job, I can steal hoodies from his room now. He says he hates it when I steal his hoodies. However, I look adorable in his hoodies. They almost go down to my knees, the perks of being 5,2. I often complain about being short; it's not so bad when you can steal hoodies, though.

The flight takes an hour, a painful hour from five thirty am. Usually, I love being in planes. I love looking out of the window and seeing the clouds below me, I love watching the sunset, and seeing everything slowly get smaller and smaller. However this journey, I was sitting next to an old guy who snores. And a nosy woman kept trying to read my texts over my shoulder. Talk about disrespect. I put my headphones in and listen to my playlist; I can hear the faint sound of my music as I drift to sleep. Bonne Nuit to me.

I come off the plane, collect my bags after what feels like forever, just standing there waiting for my neon blue suitcase. You'd think it would be painfully obvious to find. It took twenty minutes. *Twenty.* I walk outside and see him standing there waiting for me. Those warm, honey-brown eyes I've missed. Those freckles I adore. *My Luc.*

I run over to him, dropping my suitcases. I jump straight into his arms and wrap my legs around his waist. We probably look like one of those cringey airport reunions right now, and I could not care less. He tightens his arms around my waist, and I keep my head on his chest, he's so warm, and I'm so so cold.

Luc has always given the best hugs, the type that make you feel so safe. I've always been a sucker for hugs, and I think he also has. For my hugs at least. He'd never admit that, though.

I start to pull away, but he tightens his grip. I try to squirm out of his arms, he doesn't let me. Instead, he tickles me where I'm most ticklish; my sides. Why must my tickle spot be so obvious and inconvenient? Loud howls of laughter echo across the airport because apparently, I have no self-control.

Oh. My. God.

That's embarrassing. I get several disgusted stares from the Parisians. Probably not the best first impression.

I *hate* being tickled.

"Luc, we need to get to our apartment and unpack," I say, still trying to get him to stop tickling me and stop laughing ridiculously.

"Nope, just let me hug you for just a bit longer. It's been so long, My Ambre. I've missed my best friend."

My Ambre.

"Luc, it's been three weeks." Despite living a few minutes apart, since being seven, we haven't seen eachother properly for a few weeks. Which is odd considering it's an extremely small neighborhood. London is huge, our neighborhood is the opposite. We've called, texted, and he's stopped by for five minutes to say hi, but we've been completely swamped. With sorting out the moving company, sorting out our visas, not to mention the plane ticket I forgot to buy. That's why we flew separately. I'm usually the one who's great with organisation, yet somehow I forgot to buy my own ticket!

"Fine, off we go then. To our new apartment." He says with a proud smile on his face. *I'm proud of us as well.* We did it. Here we are; we made our dream come true.

A taxi pulls up and the driver helps Luc and I with our luggage. I brought as much as I could in my suitcase, everything else is being dropped off by a painfully expensive moving company. As soon as we pull out of the airport I feel giddy butterflies in my stomach. I feel like a kid waking up on Christmas day.

We pass by several cafes with elegant people going about their days despite it being only seven am, there's barely any daylight. It's crazy to think, that'll be me soon. Well after my first class. There are so many gorgeous flower shops. Bright pink roses are displayed out front. I'll be paying them a visit soon for sure.

And even a macaron shop! I've never tried a macaron. I'm ashamed honestly. It's an experience Luc and I can't wait to try out, as soon as possible!

We pull up outside the apartment complex. It's not crazy fancy, but it's adorable and perfect for two adventurous best friends. Luc grabs all the luggage whilst I stand there star-struck. I can't believe we did it. We really did it. And we're going to be okay.

"Jeez, what the hell is in this thing?" Luc groans.

"Books." I state plainly.

"Why did I even ask? Come on, let's pray they have an elevator."

"They do. I googled it." I admit proudly.

"Why am I not surprised." He smiles at me.

The main bonus of our apartment location is, it's about a five-minute walk from the Eiffel tower! So that means I can live out my dream of reading by the Eiffel tower. And now I can do it every morning if I want to. I'll be living the dream. Quite literally.

This is a dream come true; literally, *This* has been my dream since I was thirteen.

We step into the elevator, and we're greeted with three very unhappy-looking Parisians. I suppose we are crowding their home elevator with luggage. I'd be moody too, well I wouldn't but I need to be in the Parisian mindset now.

The elevator beeps at the top floor, ten floors up. I pull out two keys, Luc's is navy blue and I may have got it personalised so a french kitty wearing a beret. Mine's the same but purple. I love it.

I unlock the door, Luc opens it and we step in together...and wow. This place is beautiful. It smells of lavender and honey, immediately I feel like I'm home. The fireplace gives a homey feel, and this whole setting gives me a feeling of belonging. Across from the front door, there are two glass doors opening up to a view of the Eiffel tower in the distance. I excitedly run over and open the doors, and the view from the balcony is just, wow.

"Luc, I have no words. This place is even more beautiful in person. More than I ever could have imagined. "

"Isn't it just. I can't believe this place is all ours."

We look around the rest of the house, our small yet weirdly classy bathroom, the empty bedrooms with full-length windows, a kitchen perfect for a little human such as myself to cook some pizzas (which I will definitely be having most nights), and the open plan living room which is where we walk in, where the balcony doors are, and the other room doors are all connected to.

We're both just astonished by the place we can now call home. I never want to leave. Luc's phone rings so he steps out onto the balcony. He has that frustrated look on his face. His brows furrow, which is never a good sign. Along with a bit of disappointment. Uh oh.

"The moving company just called; they're unable to get here today. So I guess we're making do with the floor and blankets tonight."

"What! That's so annoying. We're going to be freezing, just a couple of blankets each on the floor."

"No, I'm not having you freeze; you can cuddle up to me so you're warmer. And I guess you can borrow one of my hoodies. This is a one-off. Don't get used to it."

That little smile on his face tells me he knows exactly how happy that makes me. Of course, I was going to steal a hoodie anyway, but the offer was sweet of him.

"I will not cuddle you. I'll be absolutely fine, Luc. And I mean, truth be told, I was going to steal one anyway. I appreciate the offer, though!" I explain with a smirk on my face.

"Mhm, we'll see about that. You can shush right now. You're lucky I don't take my offer back right now, princess."

Annoying him is fun. I don't always win, but it's still fun.

"You could never do that. You just love seeing how cute I look in your hoodies. Actually, I think I pull them off better than you."

"Oh, is that what you think, huh? Maybe you're the one who steals them because you're *trying* to look cute for me. Hm?"

Yeah, now he's the one smirking.

Luc point 1. Ambre point 0.

"If you don't shut up, I'm gonna sleep outside. So I'm not around you're stupid snarky comments."

"If you didn't want me to reply with a better comeback than you, you shouldn't have started it. I rest my case."

He can be very annoying sometimes. But I guess that's the price I've got to pay to have a boy as my best friend. Instead of saying something back, as I have nothing to say that would make me win this, I reach up and shake my hand through his already messy brown hair, and I mess it up even more. Payback.

"Hey, hey, no! Meany." He then puts his bottom lip out and gives me his little puppy dog eyes. That's my move, so it won't work for me. I *invented* the puppy dog eyes.

"Luc, sweetie. I invented the puppy dog eyes. That won't work on me. You should know this by now. How many times have you tried it on me?" I say, eyeing him. Luc just rolls his eyes which makes me laugh. "Okay, should we set up our "bed" for tonight?"

"Yeah. Then we can go get some food from the bakery!"

"Yeah, sure we can. Bit excited there, buddy?" I say between laughs and nudge his arm. He just frowns at me.

Luc

I honestly can't believe this day has finally come. I live in Paris. I'm getting a degree at my dream university, all with my best friend. My Mam told me to complete all my dreams, and I listened. If she could see me now, I think she would be proud. That thought keeps me going every day. I miss her. I never once believed that things would start to look up for me. I guess I was wrong.

But I owe it all to Ambre. She's the reason I've survived these past ten years. I will be forever grateful for that. I am also incredibly thankful that Paris has delicious food. This pastry is insanely good. And so is Ambre's croissant; I stole some. Oh, how I love French cafes.

"Hey, are you okay? Off in your little world." Ambre says, distracting me from my little thought bubble. Probably for the best. Being in your own head can sometimes be the worst place to be. I'm glad I'll have Ambre pecking at my head 24/7 now. Little chatterbox.

"Yeah yeah, I'm good. Just thinking."

"Oh God, don't do that." She says, sarcastically. She makes it sound like that's the worst thing I could possibly do. She's probably right, actually.

"Oh shush!" I say, laughing. "You're no better." Of course, she starts giggling like she always does. I swear we can't take each other seriously, ever. I could confess love to her, and she wouldn't take me seriously...

I have a horrible idea, and Ambre is gonna hate me. So I'm gonna do it.

"Hey, Ambre?"

"Oh God, what?" She can already tell something's up.

"I'm in love with you."

I'm clearly joking. We can't take each other seriously, so I want to see how she reacts.

Either this will go completely wrong, and she'll say she loves me back, which is impossible. Or she'll tell me to stop being a bloody idiot. Hoping it's the former. Either way, this is hilarious. The look on her face is priceless.

"I'm sorry, *you're what*? I think I misheard you. Please repeat yourself. *Right now!*" Howling laughter starts coming from me. This is hilarious. "What is this a joke? I'm genuinely confused now. Luc Bonet, explain yourself right this instant."

"Ambre de Roselle. How well do you know me?"

"Very well?"

"If you know me so well, you should be able to tell whether or not this is a joke. If you don't pick the right one, I'm going to be extremely offended, by the way."

"Well, obviously, it's got to be a joke. Right? We both know what love and a relationship would do to our friendship. And I know you would never risk that. So I'm gonna go with a joke."

"Ouch." Maybe I'm taking this too far, but messing with her is too much fun.

"Wait, you weren't serious? Were you? I'm sorry. I'm sorry, Luc."

Just laughter. So much laughter I can't breathe at this point.
"What the hell is so funny?"
"You Ambre. This is freaking hilarious. The look of panic on your face when you thought I was genuinely being serious. That will forever be imprinted in my mind."
She says nothing; she just scowls at me. Hard.
"Ambre, I'm sorry. You know I would never actually catch feelings for you. I'm not that stupid. It was just really, really funny seeing your reaction! Don't hate me." I say, trying to catch my breath between words. I put on my little pout, which we already know does not work. Worth a try.
"You are evil. I thought I hurt your feelings then! You're mean!"
"Mean? That's the best you've got? Come on, Ambre! I've taught you to insult people better than this." I'm driving her mad. It's great. The luxuries of having me as your best friend.
"I'm going to give you an option here, choose wisely. You can either shut up right now. Or you're sleeping outside. Got it?"
"Yep, sorry. Got it."
"Mhm, that's what I thought."
I probably took it a tad too far; worth it, though. The look on her face was priceless.
"And Luc, never joke about that again. I thought I'd hurt you."

"I won't, I promise! Next time I confess my love to you, it will be 100% true." I say, smiling. Ouch. Yep, she just smacked my head. And she's now walking off. "Where are you going?"

"I am going to pick up a book from the library, then I am going to read at the Eiffel tower. You are not coming with me. Unless you shush and stop making stupid jokes. Okay? Good."

"Yep, okay, got it. No more stupid jokes. I think I'll go with you and sketch while you read.

"Fine. But I will say this once, do not speak to me, especially not when I'm reading enemies to lovers, or I'll become your enemy and there will be no lovers to add on to that. Let's go!" She states and smiles sweetly. Readers are scary. I swear everyone thinks they're sweet and innocent; this one bloody isn't.

How can people read so fast? She finished an entire book. In the span of, what four hours maybe? As I said, readers are scary. Super speedy reading skills and vicious creatures.

Also, extremely high standards. Ambre was explaining what her book boyfriends are like, whatever they are? And they are nothing like real men. Yeah, I can see why she prefers them over us. Maybe I should read some romance novels and take some tips.

It is currently ten pm, and Ambre has started another book. She's halfway done already. I'm bored. No doubt she'll tell me every detail about the book and spare nothing. She will also tell me why it's the most heartbreaking story she has ever read, then do the same thing tomorrow. But all these things make Ambre, well, Ambre.

The night is freezing. We didn't choose a good time to move. And it's the worst time to have no bloody furniture. So we're both currently lying on a double quilt, with a small blanket draped across us.

It barely covers me, though, considering I'm 6,0. Ambre, on the other hand, is covered just fine. Good time to be short. She must still be cold, though. I was joking before when I told her that she would be cuddling up to me. I wish she would, though; I'd rather that than her being cold. Ambre, however, is quite the stubborn one, so if she's going to do anything tonight, it'll be staying on the other side of the quilt. All night.

I look at my phone; it's three am. I look down to see a very sleepy Ambre lying on my chest. I guess she's not so stubborn in her sleep. Of course, when she wakes up, she'll move and hope I didn't see her cuddling up to me. But I'd much rather this than her sleep on the other end of the quilt shivering.

I was going to go get something to drink, but that's not happening anymore. So she better be comfy lying on me because this hard floor is not comfortable.

I groan and sit up on the quilt, that was not a comfy bed. And the blanket is gone? No wonder I've got goosebumps. Sleeping on the floor; do not recommend. I look down to my side and my heart drops, Ambre isn't here. For God's sake. Where the hell is Ambre at this time of the morning? It's not even light out! I look around the apartment, and she's not here. Surely I should have heard her getting up. I put a hoodie on and some joggers, then head to the only place I can think of, where Ambre would be at six am. Why does she have to be such an early bird? Early birds drive me insane. Sleep is nice!

It is absolutely freezing out here. Why she would come out here willingly, in autumn, I don't know.

I can't stand being outside in the freezing cold, at six am might I add!

I was right. Here she is in all her glory. Sitting with the Eiffel tower in view on a patch of grass, with a blanket and a book. This girl is going to be the death of me.

"Ambre! What the hell! You could have told me you were coming out here. I was worried sick. Plus, you stole the bloody blanket!" She smiles up at me like she somehow finds this amusing. "Ambre, it's not funny. I woke up, and you were gone. I was terrified. You can't just leave at six in the morning and not tell me where you're going. At least leave a note."

"Aw, I'm sorry, Luc. You just looked so cute fast asleep! You were drooling too. I didn't wanna wake you! I'm very sorry for stealing the blanket, in my defence, aren't you always too hot? I'm sure it's colder out here than in there."

I don't say anything in return. I just stand there with my arms crossed. I'm not even going to argue her on the blanket, I won't win, but does she really want to go there? How cute I looked in my sleep whilst drooling? Let the games begin.

"Yeah, I'm sure I looked adorable! You know you also drool in your sleep! Yeah, I noticed when I woke up at three in the morning to see you all cuddled up to me! What was that about you saying that you wouldn't cuddle up to me, hm?" She's death glaring at me. Oh well.

"Got nothing to say now, princess? Do ya?" I say, giving her a little wink.

"Do *not* call me princess! I've told you how ridiculous it is."

"That's all you've got to say? Okay, guess we know who won that round." I give her another little wink just to annoy her that little bit more.

"I'm heading back to the apartment. We start classes today. I don't want to be late."

Then she's gone.

⚘ *Chapter 2* ⚘

Ambre

I'm in my first class; I should be excited, right? But all I can think of is what Luc said before.

I know I was cuddled up to him; I woke up in his arms. I had hoped that he wouldn't see me. I thought I'd gotten away with it when I left super early. But I guess not; he saw me. That's awkward.

How am I meant to face him later? I'd told him earlier that day that that would not happen. And it did. This furniture better hurry up. That will not happen again.

I know I shouldn't react this way, but he's my best friend. And before you know it, cuddles will turn into kisses, kisses turn into feelings, and feelings cause heartbreak. And heartbreak would ruin our friendship! I won't let that happen. It's always been Ambre and Luc; nothing could ever separate us.

I know for a fact that if feelings were to develop from either of us, that would ruin our friendship. One would constantly feel nervous rather than having fun like you should when with friends. I also know that I am totally overthinking this. I have always been one to over analyse everything, and I mean *everything*. Am I overreacting to this?

"Ambre de Roselle? Miss de Roselle, please answer the question now." Oh, this isn't good. I wasn't listening. It's my first day. This will not leave a good impression.

"I'm sorry, Madam. Can you repeat the question?" Not that I'll know the answer.

"So you weren't listening? I don't want this again, Miss de Roselle. Understood? Students here study hard and pay attention in classes! Something you were not doing. I will come back to you afterwards. Pay attention now, or you will not be welcome in my class."

I'm going to go ahead and burst my thought bubble. I need to pay attention now; this professor scares me.

"Yes, Madam. My apologies."

I spend the rest of class taking so many notes that my hand cramps. I'm going to need to put in so much extra effort now. I want my professor to like me. I have a craving for academic validation. Study night it is.

 If I work hard enough, I can get to the top of my class, and my professor will love my writing. Hopefully.

Class finishes, and I'm relieved I no longer have to be around that professor. But now I have to face Luc. I told him we could meet up after class and get some lunch. I can't face him now; I don't know what to say. Do I bring it up? Do I apologise? Do I pretend I didn't spend the night cuddling up to him as if he were my boyfriend? There's no right answer here!

"Hey, girl! You look like you need a coffee. Wanna come with? I was in that class with you. God, that professor is harsh! I think she needs a drink!"

I have no idea who this girl is. She's gorgeous, though. She has beautiful light-brown skin and dark brown and curly hair. Then to top it all off, she has green eyes. Dark green forest-like eyes. She's perfect.

"I'm just stressing about class, that's all. But, yes, I do need some caffeine! If someone just took that professor out drinking for a night, maybe then she'll loosen up a bit!" My comment makes us both laugh. I think I've found myself a new friend.

"Ambre, right? I'm Caroline."

"Yep, that's me. It's nice to finally have someone to talk to who's a girl! And who shares my love for writing, of course."

"Wwww spill girly, is he hot? And duh! Writing is the best, who wouldn't love it?"

"Well, he's been my best friend since I was about three. So I'm just going to keep my mouth shut and let you see for yourself if he's "hot".

"Okay, denial. I see you. You totally think he's hot, but refuse to admit it to yourself. It's okay; I love playing matchmaker. Oh. My. God. You should write a story about your love story! How you were childhood friends, then fell madly in love. I love that trope. Please write it, or I'm going to have to. And if I write it, I'll let everyone know you have been in love with him all along. And was just too scared to admit it."

"No, no, no. I have never been in love with him. Ever. I could never see anything happening with him. We've known each other our whole lives. That would be way too weird. Honestly, girl, he's all yours if you want him.

"Nope, he's yours. You don't see it yet, but you will definitely fall in love with each other. I just know it."

"Okay, enough of this talk! I thought we were getting coffee. Let's go! My feet are getting tired of standing."

"This conversation is to be continued. You ain't getting away from it that quick girl." I laugh.

I've known this girl for what, five minutes? I already know we're going to be good friends. She seems fun and genuine. She doesn't seem fake like some people are. That's why Luc and I usually just stick with each other, just us.

"This place is nice!"

"I know, right? I come here all the time, every morning before classes, and on my way home. Yeah, I'm pretty much addicted to caffeine at this point."

"Aren't we all," I say, laughing.

"So! Back to our previous conversation,"

"Oh, God, please, no."

"Yes. Okay, so, you've like never kissed him?"

"What? God no! If that happened, I don't think we could face each other again."

"Never wanted to? Because even if you've never wanted to kiss him, he has definitely wanted to kiss you."

"Nope, nope, nope. Never wanted to and never will. And what in the world would bring you to the conclusion that he's wanted to kiss me? I highly doubt that."

"I mean, just look at you. No guy could ever be friends with you and not once want to kiss you. You're like the type of girl that turns heads. All the guys will be jealous of him for even being friends with you. You have dark blue eyes, which are so enticing. You have super cute hazelnut brown curls. I'll bet he loves it. In fact, I'll bet every guy loves it."

"You say all this, but it's not often I get hit on."

"Hmmm, I wonder why? Because all the guys think you're taken, boo!"

"Huh, I've never actually thought of that. I get that boys can be intimidated by Luc, but I'd never have thought they assumed we were together."

"Yeah, they definitely think you're together. So his name's Luc? Let's insta stalk him. See if he *is* hot." Jokes on her; he doesn't post. Luc is a very private person.

"Luc Bonet? He's the only Luc I can find that follows your account. Huh, he has no posts. Aw, that's a shame. It's fine, though; I'll just facetime you, and you can show me. Oh, speaking of facetime, let me put my number in your phone so we can facetime!"

"Yeah, sure, one problem, I doubt he'd let me show him. He's quite a private person." I pass her my phone and let her give me her number; maybe we could facetime. I just know Luc won't let me show him.

"So he's a hot, mysterious guy. Who's also your best friend? Sorry, remind me quickly, why *the heck* aren't you together!?" I can't help but laugh at her dramatics.

"We won't date each other, friendship only between us! You can not convince me otherwise. Maybe *you* should try it with him; it seems like he's your dream guy."

"Nuh-uh. I could never date a guy who clearly already has a future wifey. Okay, so I guess there's no convincing you, for now, but just you wait!"

"Yep, definitely not going to be convincing me anytime soon."

"Okay, well, time shall tell. Don't even try to deny it. Anyway! Tomorrow night a couple of friends and I are having a small gathering! At our house. I have two roommates. Lucie and Alexandre, he hates being called that, so call him Alex. There is *plenty* of space for you to join, and I'm sure they wouldn't mind if you wanted to bring Luc. Will you come? Please? I'll text you the address!"

"Oh my gosh, yes! It's gonna be a piece of work trying to convince Luc. But I'm sure I'll manage. I can't wait! This is going to be epic!" I really, really hope I can convince Luc to come through.

"Yay! Okay, so I have a class in five minutes, and I will definitely be late. Totally worth it, though! I convinced you! Anyways see you tomorrow, boo!" She says with a grin on her face.

"See you tomorrow, girl!"

I like Caroline, I think she's probably a bit much for Luc, but I love her. Her energy is phenomenal.

We ended up meeting for lunch in this little diner near campus. I loved the cafe, but Luc insisted this place is better.

"Okay, so don't kill me,"

"What've you done now?"

I sip my coffee slowly, trying to stall time.

"So, I may have told this girl from class that we would meet with her and her friends Saturday... She's so lovely, though! You'll love her!" *Or maybe he'll hate her.* "We're going to have fun."

"I've got plans." He says.

"Doing what?" I asked, surprised.

"Anything but that." He says with a flat smile.

I roll my eyes. "Well, I'm not letting you stay in, we're going out, and that's final."

"Fine. But I'm not conversing with your new little friends."

"Luc, come on. Try to get to know them. Maybe then you'll have more than one friend. Which is me." I say with a laugh.

"Oh, you can shut up right now, princess."

Luc moves over to me and quickly grabs me.

"No, no, what are you doing?"

"Payback." Then before I can defend myself, he attacks me with tickles. Torture.

"Luc, Stop! This is pure torture. You're so mean!" I can hardly get my words out without having to stop for air. "Have mercy! I'm going to pass out!"

"God, you're dramatic, princess. Always have been."

"Yes, but I'm amazing at it."

"That's true. Maybe acting should be your profession instead of writing!"

"Oh shush, as if I'd survive even thirty seconds on stage. I'm gonna stick to writing, thanks though!"

"That's true; you'd probably come running to me, asking me to save you. As always." He says with that knowing smirk on his face. So I just nudge him with my elbow. "Ouch! So violent Madam de Roselle. You're going to end up killing somebody with that!" I hide a slight smile. That boy.

"Shut up. Right, we still need to order some food. We've been sitting in this booth for about twenty minutes and still haven't ordered! I bet people are annoyed." Several people give me daggers, I feel the nerves knot in my stomach due to their attention.

"Oh well, screw the people. Pretend they're not there. You worry too much about their validation." It's true; I do care about others' validation. More so than my own.

The waitress walks toward our table. Time to make our order! Wait, will she speak English? My french is still a little rusty.

"Hi, could I please get the margarita pizza? And a glass of orange juice with that, please. Thank you so much." She doesn't talk or say anything to me. I found it a bit rude since she was just eyeing up Luc the whole time.

"Yeah, and I'll just have the spaghetti, please. Mocha with that, please. Thanks."

"Anything on that, sir?"

"Yeah," He zones in on her nametag. He always does this wherever we are. "I'll have some cheese, please, Louise."

"Is that everything?" She asks with a glint in her eyes whilst checking Luc out.

"That's it. Thanks," I reply with a firm tone. She's clearly trying to flirt with Luc. Then she rolls her eyes at me. Real mature.

"I'll leave my number on the receipt for you." She says, then winks at him as she walks off. What the hell?

"Actually," She turns her head back to me and does not look happy. "he's not available. Yeah, we've been together for five years. I'm sorry, love. I know he's gorgeous." I give her a warming smile. Can't be mad at someone with a sweet smile, right?

She scoffs and walks away. As she should. Was I a bit out of order there? I mean, yeah, sorta. But she seemed sly and rude; I was simply helping out my best friend.

"I'm so gorgeous, am I?" He smirks. This is fantastic. Just fantastic.

"I'm sorry, Luc. I don't know what that was for. I'm sorry. She just seemed rude! I was trying to help you. That's all. She's definitely not good enough for my best friend. And for the love of God, stop reading nametags! They always think you're flirting!"

"It's funny, though! Plus, I couldn't miss that chance; it all rhymed! Honestly, princess, I didn't mind you looking out for me." He says with a shrug. Also, bloody smirking.

"What? Luc, what are you smirking at now?"

"You. Ambre de Roselle, was jealous."

"Jealous? Me? As if."

"Don't even try to deny it. So is today our anniversary?"

"Oh, my God, please shut up."

"You so were jealous! Trying to keep me all for yourself, were ya now? Well, don't worry, I'm all yours, baby."

"In your dreams."

"Or in yours." He winks. He flipping winks at me.

"No, thank you. I'll stick to dreaming about my book boyfriends; they're better."

"I'm hotter."

My laughter fills the air. So how does one respond to their cocky best friend?

"What? What is so funny about that, hm? I am totally hotter."

"Now that is definitely in your dreams. Nobody will ever compare to fictional men. My standards are raised through the roofs."

"Nope, I'm still hotter. You're just too scared to admit it."

"Keep dreaming, Luc."

"I will." He says confidently. This boy.

"Mhm, you do that." He pouts, which he thinks works.

After a good twenty minutes, our food arrives! From a different waitress, thank the Lord.

"Oh wow, this food is drool-worthy." I agree with him there.

"It sure is. Be quiet now; I'm gonna demolish this in silence."

"Okay, you do that. Crazy little thing."

"Shhhh" This comes out muffled, as, as I said, I am demolishing this.

Luc

Once we've finished our food, we just sit in a food coma. That was hella good.

"Are you ready to head back then? I've got a class in about an hour and need to grab some stuff from the apartment."

"Yep, I'm ready. If I can move. Carry me?"

"Come on, drama queen." I say, laughing. She's so dramatic. I leave the money on our table and a little extra because that food was phenomenal.

We both just flop onto the couch when we get home. Which finally arrived earlier, along with our other furniture. No more sleeping on the floor. And now, with all these boxes, the place is a mess. Ambre's probably going to sort it all out to her liking afterwards. Fine by me.

"I'm gonna grab my stuff and head to class. Meet you at the cafe for a coffee after, yeah?"

It's a bit early, but I can't be late for this class. They're apparently extremely strict here. Expecting everyone to be on time. How can they actually think that's gonna happen? We're university students, most of which are either drunk, high or sleep-deprived. Or all three.

"Yeah, sure. Have fun in class! Tell me all the details afterwards." She says in a sing-song voice.

"Byeee, Ambre."

⚔ Chapter 3 ⚔

Luc

This class is hectic. I guess I assumed everyone was going to be classy snobs. But, no, the professor is ten minutes late, and a bunch of students are sitting on the desks in the corner drinking. Others making out. Lovely.

Fire science is my degree. I haven't told Ambre yet; I want it to be a surprise. She'll be proud.

My Papa was a firefighter, he died saving people in a crash. A commercial plane lost control, crashed and landed in a dynamic field, causing a massive fire. Five hundred people died that day. Some were unfortunate enough to be near the accident when it happened. Many of those people were also the emergency services. My Papa, being the hero, runs into that fire, trying to save everyone. He saved thirteen people. Thirteen. But he couldn't save himself.

He died a hero. He'll *always* be my hero. And my dream is to make him proud. I will make him proud and carry on his legacy. I will make my Mam proud.

The professor shows up. What twenty minutes late by now? Yeah. So not much learning is happening today.

"Good afternoon, Ladies and Gentlemen! I'm so sorry for being late. I clicked stop instead of snooze. It happens to all of us, right? And then I needed coffee, or I would have been a zombie teaching you." He doesn't seem to care all that much, to be honest. But at least he's chill.

"So! Shall we start with introductions?" No, no, no, no, no.

"You! Brown hair, freckles. Name?"

You've got to be bloody joking me.

"Luc."

"And do you have a last name, Monsieur Luc?"

"Bonet"

"Wow, very french! You don't sound french, though. You're new to Paris, yes?"

"Yes, just moved here. My Mam's french, so that's where the name's from."

"Ah, I see. Well, Luc, I would love to hear more about you. You have sparked my interest! Any specific reason as to why you're taking fire sciences?"

"Sparked my interest, I guess," I say, quoting him with a flat smile.

"Okay then, you don't seem overly fond of me. We'll change that. Don't you worry." He says while laughing it off. And I'm not exactly thrilled to have sparked his interest.

The class, which ended up only thirty minutes, felt like a lifetime. Rather than teaching me something valuable, he just chatted all the bleeding lesson.

Class is over now, so I'll meet Ambre back at the cafe and no doubt she'll talk my head off about something. As always.

"Hey! Luc, right? I'm Lucie; I'm in your class." Why, why, why do people keep talking to me?

"Yeah, that's me."

"I'm a good friend of Caroline's. She mentioned that you and some Ambre would be joining us tomorrow night. I wasn't sure who you were, but I knew it was you after hearing your name. Very unique."

"I believe we are joining you, yeah. I'm not coming by choice, though. I'm coming for Ambre."

"Oh, okay. So is Ambre a girlfriend or?" She stops waiting for me to continue.

"Ambre is not a girlfriend, no. But if that's your way of asking me out, it's going to be a pass for today. Sorry, not a big dater."

"Oh no, no, I sort of get that vibe from you anyways. Just you know, doing some background checks for future reference." She says jokingly.

I mean, she's not bad to look at with those big brown eyes and purple streaks through her bleach-blonde hair, and she seems to be a decent human being. But as I told her, I'm not a big dater. I've had the odd girlfriend in high school, but it never lasted. I was either "Too closed off" or "way too friendly with that girl", mainly just petty girls being intimidated by Ambre.

"See you tomorrow then."

"Yeah, definitely! I look forward to it. And hey, if you ever want a new friend in this big city, here's my number." I get handed a piece of paper with her number. And with that, she's off. Lucie, I'm somewhat intrigued by you.

Ambre

"Luc Bonet!! Where have you been?? I've been sitting here waiting for thirty minutes!"

"My bloody professor wouldn't shut up, and he was twenty minutes late to the lecture! He let us out ten minutes late, and then some girl, who is apparently close to your new friend, started speaking to me."

"What you got in your hand? Just casually holding a piece of paper?" Normal Luc things, I suppose.

"Oh no, Lucie gave me her number in case I wanted a friend."

Yeah, she definitely *just* wants to be friends. Is he stupid?

"Oh cool, who's Lucie then?"

"That girl, the one who's friends with that girl you spoke to. Caroline, I think it was."

"I'm not so sure she wants just to be friends, Luc. But I mean, go for it, I guess. Just don't forget about me." I half-joke.

Luc laughs. "Oh, be quiet, Ambre. I told her I'm not much of a dater. You can stop being jealous now." He smirks.

I gasp dramatically. "As if I would be jealous! You need to stop flattering yourself, Luc Bonet."

"Yeah yeah, okay. Wink wink"

"Luc, please tell me you did not just say 'wink wink', my Lord, you are cringey."

Luc just laughs. "Me!? *I'm* the cringey one? Says the girl who reads romcoms for a living."

"I am offended! How dare you diss my amazing books. You play cringey love songs on the guitar! So hush." He exaggerates his shock.

"Because you request them! Gosh, Ambre." I swear the Parisians must think we're on something.

"Gosh, Luc! Okay, now I'm hungry and tired. Hometime, come on!" I start to leave the cafe leaving Luc to follow along.

"I'm coming, I'm comi-" He whines until he pauses suddenly, "It's raining!"

I love rain. I'm a pluviophile.

"Let's dance," I state. And it's happening, whether he likes it or not.

"I think not." I plead with my eyes. But, you see, *my* puppy dog eyes work.

"Fine. Not here though, c'mon, let's get out of here." And with that, he's running. And he's bloody fast.

"Luc! Wait for me!" I rasp between breaths. I failed PE if you couldn't tell.

He swiftly comes to a stop for me. "Hurry up, slowpoke." He smirks. Damn you, Luc.

"Oh, I apologise; not everyone got an A* in PE!! I don't do running, Connard." Connard translates to some swear word in English. I learned that from Caroline in English lit today; she kept swearing at Beau in French. It was hilarious.

"What did you just call me, Ambre de Roselle?" I begin laughing; I don't think he knows what that means. Well, I hope he doesn't know what that means.

Luc swoops me into his arms and carries me bridal style; he knows. "I'm gonna throw you into the lake." He better not.

"Luc, I swear to God, if you so much as take me near that freaking lake, I will kill you! Put me down right now!"

"Make me then." I'm going to commit murder.

"As if you'd even know where there's a lake here.

"For a matter of fact, I do."

"Go on then, name it."

"Bassin de la Villette. Or, of course, there's the river Seine. Did you forget about that one, princess?" *Uh oh.*

"Luc, you're running through Paris, *carrying me* whilst it's throwing it down with rain. I'm getting frostbite. I want to go home." I whine.

"I'll keep you warm, princess." He remarks with a smirk.

"One day, I'm going to wipe that smirk off your face!!"

"Go on then."

To my luck, he took us home. I was not thrown into the lake. I glare at him. "Thank you. I suppose."

"Well, we got home faster than you would've with your slow little legs."

"Shut up, and for the last time, put me down! There's no need for you to be carrying me now."

"Okay, princess, have it your way."

"Thank y- *OW!* What the hell was that for? You dropped me!"

"You said to put you down, So I did." He declares between laughs.

"I hate you."

"Sure you do, princess." Luc winks again. I swear he's trying to provoke me.

"Shut up." He's annoying and knows how to get a reaction. With that, I head into the apartment building, closing the door behind me. Luc says something, but all I hear are muffled words coming from behind the door.

Opening the door, I ask him, "what was that, sorry? I don't understand Mumbled words." I glare at him with a sly smile.

Luc rolls his eyes. "I said you forgot about the dancing, princess." He distracted me from the dancing! And now I'm all wet and need a shower.

"This isn't over, Luc! You shall dance with me. And it's going to be the best day of your life."

"Mhm, definitely. We'll see about that. "

"It's happening! Anyway, I'm going to get a shower because *somebody* dropped me on the cold, wet floor."

"Want a guest?" Luc questions with a smirk. This boy, oh my God.

"Luc, for once in your life, rather than being a sarcastic idiot, just don't speak! It is not hard. Try it sometime!"

"Who says I was being sarcastic?" Here he goes again.

"That stupid smirk on your face tells me all I need to know. And if you weren't joking for some reason, no, Luc, you can not join me." I huff.

"I'll take it as a pass for today, then? Maybe next time, hey?"

Rather than giving him the reaction he so clearly desires, I leave him outside, and I go get a shower. Because I'm cold and gross. And I want to get into warm pyjamas and then read. Why is Paris so cold?

🗼 Chapter 4 🗼

Luc

I've been sitting on this bench watching the rain for about forty minutes. No joke. I'm absolutely drenched, but it's worth it. Rain has always been peaceful to me, comforting even. I should definitely head inside now, my shirt has become see-through, and my hair is dripping. The sun has begun to set; I can't believe Ambre is missing this. The pinks and oranges mixing together creates this dream-like allusion.

 If I had all my painting equipment, I would capture this moment because it's beautiful. Not many things in life are beautiful, but rain and sunsets are the most beautiful things this world has ever given us. How poetic of me. See, I can be genuine when I feel like it.

I leave trails of raindrops along the floor and up the stairs, right to the top floor.

Walking in, I'm greeted with a home. A real home with furniture, pictures, of course a bookshelf and some candles.

Sure enough, Ambre has arranged all our furniture into the places she believes perfect. There's still more to unpack but she's got the majority.

The most exciting, we now have beds! And couches! No more sleeping on the floor, thank God. And now I've got my own space to paint.

I hear a soft singing voice coming from the bathroom; I guess I'm not showering yet, then.

I fetch my sketchbook and open it up. I've been working on this piece for a while. It's sort of a mix of everything Ambre and Luc. Music notes scattered all over to resemble Ambres singing and my guitar playing. Some pencils and paintbrushes to show my love for art, books for Ambre, and the Eiffel tower resembling our new journey.

Of course, I'll add to it. I'm covering every last bit of this paper with art. I feel like simply sketching those things won't give this piece the life it needs. So I'm adding paint at the end.

I'm hoping to gift this to Ambre for her birthday. I don't usually let people see my art. It's something for me. But I figured for Ambre's nineteenth in January, she might like something more personal.

The bathroom door opens as I'm adding a few extra touches. I quickly put my sketchbook in the drawer; it can stay there until Ambre goes to sleep.

Ambre comes out of the bathroom, still singing. She jumps back when she sees me. "Jeez, Luc! You scared me! You could have been a murderer!"

"Because a murderer would *definitely* be sitting at our kitchen table?"

"Hey, for all I know, you could have been there waiting for me so you could kill me."

"Ambre, I'm sure any murderer smart enough to get into our apartment unnoticed is also smart enough to hide." Ambre scowls at me.

"Just a thought," I add, shrugging my shoulders.

"Okay, anyway, the bathroom is free. Looks like you need it." She says, looking me up and down.

"*Excuse* me, I've been waiting for you to finish your spa session. Seriously, who takes that long to shower? Also, you're odd you know, who half unpacks and *then* showers? "

"Luc, hunny, a spa session would take *much* longer." She states, ignoring my last comment whilst rolling her eyes.

I enjoy watching firefighter documentaries before sleeping. It's bound to help with coursework. And it's sort of nice to feel closer to my Papa. I miss my Papa. He was a great man. A really great man.

It's ten pm, so Ambre should be bingeing another series or sleeping.

I make my way to Ambre's room and knock lightly; I don't want to wake her if she's already asleep. No answer. Slowly I creak open the door, and there she is, fast asleep. I make my way to Ambre, this probably looks creepy as hell, but I just admire her. She's at peace when she's sleeping. The only time when her mind isn't running all over the place.

Ambre doesn't give herself enough credit; she's so strong. She still has her Mum, but her Dad wasn't ever there. Most of the time, Ambre was the one looking after Ami while her Mum worked late. Ami is fourteen now, so she can be home alone for longer.

Honestly, I think that affected Ambre more than she'd like to admit. Not having your father there is *hard*, especially at a young age. *I know*. Even though I had Eric, he was never a good stepfather. I wouldn't even call him a stepfather; he doesn't deserve that title.

When my Mam died, he got worse. The drinking was more frequent, and the punishments got more physical. Those memories haunt me, and Ambre, for that matter.

She acts tough as if nothing bothers her like it doesn't play on her mind constantly. But I know Ambre. All she's ever truly wanted is to be loved and to feel safe. Her Dad made her feel the opposite of all that. I won't ever let anyone hurt her again; as long as Ambre is with me, she's safe.

Moving a loose strand of hair behind her ear, I whisper, "goodnight, princess." She claims to hate when I call her princess, but I won't stop. Because as much as I love annoying the hell out of her, she's always been, my princess. Graceful, kind, so empathetic it hurts, beautiful.

I close the door, grab my sketchbook from the drawer, and head back to bed.

Bonne Nuit Paris.

I wake up to the sound of loud banging on my door. What the hell?

"I'm trying to sleep. Bugger off, it's Saturday."

"Wake up! It's eleven am!" That's not Ambre's voice?

I drag myself out of bed, throw on some sweats and a hoodie, and open the door.

"Who the hell are you?"

"Omg! So *you're* Luc. "

"Yes, and *you* are?"

"I'm honestly offended that you don't know who I am. Well, I know all about you! Ambre always talks about you."

"Ah, you must be Caroline. Ambre mentioned you were... energetic. You sound like you've had ten cups of coffee this morning."

"Five, actually. And yes, I'm Caroline. Duh."

"Okay, Caroline, why are you banging on my door at eleven am on a Saturday?"

"Because! Ambre takes forever to get ready, and I'm showing her all the best places to shop today. Girls day! Unless, of course, you want to join. I mean, we need to get you a more chic outfit for tonight anyways." She adds, looking me up and down. Scratch that; she's *judging* my outfit. What's wrong with my outfit? It's a black hoodie and grey sweats, simple.

"What's wrong with my outfit?"

"It's just so, blah! Like, we need to spice you up a bit. You're currently giving off depressed emo vibes."

"Okay, and? Maybe I like depressing emo vibes."

"You do, you boo. I'm just saying, if you want to appear more approachable, let me help you! I'm great with fashion. Also, I've already totally grilled Ambre; it's your turn. I need as much info as possible, so I can one day write your love story."

"My what? What do you mean by my love story?"

"Nothing. Anyways, you coming?"

"Fine, let me sort my hair out and change into jeans. I'll be out in five."

"Oh, I'd say leave it. Girls go wild for the messy hair look." I roll my eyes and retreat to my room. Today is going to be painful. Once Ambre is ready, we leave to go shopping. I want to die. Why did I agree to this? Ambre wears a tight black skirt and a woolly jumper to keep her warm and knee-high boots. She's good with picking outfits.

Caroline and Ambre don't stop talking on the way to the metro. Then we ride the train to La Vallee Village. Why they couldn't have chosen a closer place that isn't nearly an hour away, I don't know. All they talk about the whole way there are books and how hot the fictional people are. Then what clothes they're going to wear or buy. I regret coming on this trip.

"Okay, besties! Where to start?" She asks as soon as we step off the train. She's so freaking energetic. She and Ambre are made for each other.

"Home?" I suggest.

"Luc, sweetie, we haven't even started yet! Ambs, where shall we go? Dress shop? Luc, you can be the judge. I'm sure you won't mind gawking at Ambre in a dress anyways." The hell? She knows we're best friends, right?

"Care, I've told you! We're *friends*!"

"Yes, you have told me that, but I don't believe you; I can feel the chemistry!"

"Don't become a scientist then; you can't *feel* chemistry." I chide, rolling my eyes.

"Is he always so smug and annoying?"

"Yeah, you'll get used to it; just ignore him."

Ambre pulls me aside from Caroline, "Can you please be nice? I like this girl. She's the first friend I've made!" No, no, I can not.

"I'll be nice if she doesn't annoy me."

"Well, Caroline is literally *your* definition of annoying, but she's my new friend, and I adore her. Do not scare her off!"

"Fine."

"You two done flirting? The dress shop is over here! Come on!" I
roll my eyes, and that gets me a glare from Ambre. So we follow
Caroline to the dress shop. How fun. Not.

"Oh my gosh! Look at this red dress! Caroline, this would look
gorgeous on you!"

"That's beautiful! But honestly, I'm more of a dark green kind of
girl; it compliments my eyes. You, however, would look so hot in
that dress. Go try it on, Luc and I will judge!"

"Okay! I'm finding you a gorgeous green dress after, though."
She says, walking into the dressing room.

Leaving me alone with Caroline. Great.

"Right, now we're alone. Spill."

"Spill?"

"Yes! God, Luc. What's the deal with you and Ambre?"

"We're just best friends, always have been."

"I'm not blind. You two, maybe, but I'm not. The way your face
lights up when talking to her. Or the way her eyes sparkle when
talking about you. I know you're *just friends,* but I've heard that
one too many times. If you don't admit it, one of you will end
up heartbroken. So Luc, what's it going to be?"

As she finishes her sentence, Ambre walks out of the dressing
room in that knee-length flowy red dress. She looks beautiful.
God, I wish I could capture this moment. But, as if she had the

same thought, Caroline gets her camera out and snaps a picture of Ambre.

Ambre, however, doesn't realise she's in her own little world, twirling and all. I just admire. That is until I'm snapped back to reality when a bright flash catches my attention. You're freaking joking. Caroline just caught me staring. And she took a picture.

"Delete that right now," I demand under my breath.

"Luc, sweetie, this is proof. No way am I deleting this. I'll show it on your wedding day." She adds with a wink. I swear if she shows Ambre, I'm screwed. The way I was looking at her... friends probably *shouldn't* look at friends that way.

"Caroline, I'm begging you. Don't show Ambre."

"We'll see." she smirks. I'm screwed.

"Guys? What do you think? Honestly, I love it."

"Girl, You look hotter than the fire in hell!"

"Yeah, what she said." How does one compliment his best friend without seeming flirty?

"Yes then? Okay, I'm going to get it!"

"Let me buy it for you."

"Luc, as much as I appreciate that, I'm okay, thank you."

"Please, it can be a congratulatory gift."

Ambre laughs. "What are you congratulating me for?"

"For pursuing your dream of living in Paris and just being you."

"Luc, you know I can't let you do that. Thank you, though."

"Girl, let him buy you the dress! For goodness sake. I wish I had someone spoiling me. The boy wants to get you the dress, so let him."

"Yeah, I agree with Caroline. Wow, I never thought those words would come out of my mouth."

"Oh, shut up." Caroline nudges me.

"Nope. Still not happening. I'm gonna go get changed now. Then I'll pay, and we can find Care a dress." Then she's gone again.

"You're still going to get the dress, aren't you?"

"Yes, I am. When she comes out, I'll just snatch the dress and quickly pay for it."

"Or better yet, go get another dress off the rack? Duh."

"Right, yeah, that would make a little more sense."

"Good, hurry! I'll distract her."

I run over to the section we were in; yes, her dress is here! I grab the dress in Ambres size and head over to the counter.

"Bonjour Madame. Je voudrais acheter cette robe rouge." I studied a little before coming here.

She doesn't speak to me, which I'd rather. I'm not looking to start a whole conversation in French. She scans the dress, and it comes to ninety-five euros. Wow, that's expensive. That explains why Ambre wouldn't let me buy it for her. Oh well, I'm getting it. So she'll just have to deal with it. She packages the dress up. I pay and quickly head back to the dressing rooms.

"I'm back!"

"Took you long enough! Quick! She'll come out in a second. Go to that side, get to the *other* side!"

"Okay, okay, chill!"

"Sorry that took me so long; the strings at the back are confusing! Care? Where's Luc?"

"Surprise!"

"Surprise what? Why are you hiding?" Right, she doesn't know about the dress. My "surprise" probably didn't make much sense. Yep, Carolines rolling her eyes. I hand Ambre the bag.

"Luc, I told you no! Oh my God, thank you. Thank you so much." She throws herself into my arms. I hear another click in the background. Caroline and her damn pictures. "Really, Luc, thank you." She says, looking at me this time.

"You're very welcome, princess. Right, you two go get that green dress, I saw this place I want to go to, so I'll meet you both at the metro."

"I thought we could grab some lunch here!" Carolineand Ambre pout.

"Fine, meet you at the cafe then." With that, I leave. I do not like dress shops.

A few shops down, there's this tattoo studio; I want to get flames done on my back. Resembling my new journey and all my Dad did for those people.

I wanted to get something done for my Mam as well. So I got her favourite flower up my arm: roses, with "Mama" written underneath them. I always used to call her Mama. I got bullied for it. Eric also told me I *had* to grow out of it. I never questioned him; I was scared. So I started calling her Mam instead.

Ambre and Caroline are waiting at the cafe for me, probably wondering what took me so long.

"Where have you been?" They both question. Until their eyes go down to my plastic-covered arm.

"You got a freaking tattoo?" Ambre questions. She looks excited but also confused.

"I did. And I love them."

"Two surprises in one day? Gosh. Wait, *them?*"

"There's another on my back. I'll show you later."

"Okay." She smiles.

"So, is this a party or just meeting friends?" I question Caroline.

"I mean, it was just going to be a few friends, but they invited more friends. So I guess it's both! The girlies are all dressing up, though."

"I sure as hell hope you don't expect me to show up in a suit."

"Chill. No, we don't." Then, rolling her eyes, she turns to Ambre, "Is he always so dramatic?"

"Yes. Yes, he is."

"I am not! You, Miss Ambre, are the dramatic one."

"Mhm."

After having some food and coffee, we decide to head home. Thankfully.

⚑ *Chapter 5* ⚑

Ambre

Gathering of friends, she said. Well, that didn't go according to plan. Luc is probably dying inside right about now. I, however, am buzzing.

I'm about to meet so many new people. Of course, some of them will be my new friends, as they're Care's friends. God, I hope they like me. But, wait, no, what if I embarrass myself? Okay, I wasn't overthinking before, but now I am.

This house is so crowded, about forty-five people? That's not awful, but it's definitely not a small gathering.

"Girl, stop. I can practically hear those thoughts running through your head. Tell them to shut the hell up so we can have a good time."

I laugh at her boldness. "Thanks, Care. I'll try to shut them up now. Love you."

"I love you too, boo! Come on, let's go mingle!" Laughing along, I follow her.

People are taking shots on the tables, some are playing video games in the front room, and others are dancing; I want to dance!

"Care!" This music is deafening! "Caroline!"

"YES? SORRY, I CAN'T HEAR YOU VERY WELL!" She screams, dragging me into the next room.

Caroline slams the door, blocking out that insane music. We're now met with three others. One girl, she's pretty, she's insanely pretty. Some guy whom I have never met. He's cute, dirty blonde messy hair. I've never been one for blondes; he pulls it off, though. He's got that chilled-back, surfer boy look. Captivating blue eyes, greenish as well. Then we have...Luc?

"Luc! I was wondering where you got off to. I was worried."

"I'm safe, chill, Ambre. Don't stress. Are you okay?"

"Yes, I'm fine. Care and I have been walking about. Now we're here." I add shrugging. I'm just confused; why would Luc sit with some random people?

The silence grows awkward; nobody speaks. "Okay then." Care chimes in, of course. "Introduction time! Ambre, this is Lucie and Alex. My two besties!"

Lucie. This is Lucie? The girl that wanted to be friends with Luc, a girl that pretty definitely does not want to just be friends with a guy as hot as Luc. Did I just call Luc hot? Never mind, not the point.

I feel unnecessarily nervous and start speaking really fast. I can't help it; that's what happens when I'm scared!

"It's so good to finally meet you, Lucie. Luc spoke of you. You seem lovely, and you're gorgeous, by the way. Alex! I've never met you, hi! You're also gorgeous." I talk at an unnatural pace for the entire time I'm talking. I ramble when I'm nervous. *Oh my God,* I did not just call some random guy gorgeous the first time meeting him. Can I die now?

"Well, hello there, Ambre. Thanks for the compliment; it's not often I get called gorgeous by beautiful women like you." Alex winks.

That was kind of hot.

Lucie gives Alex an amused look, then turns to me, "He's not wrong; you're beautiful. Care speaks so highly of you! We're hyped to meet you. I've already met Luc; we're in the same fir-" Lucie gets cut off when Luc puts a hand over her mouth. And whispers something to her. Is it just me, or are they *really close?* Lucie nods in agreement. What the hell is Luc telling this girl he's not telling me?

She carries on, "We met in class. Luc seems amazing. So I have no doubt you are too."

"Care and I first met outside of class. Our professor was so bloody miserable. Then she called me out in front of the class because I looked like I wasn't paying attention! First day as well. I wanted to die right there. I always dread her class now." Care, and I laugh.

Care, Lucie, and I dance around the house while singing along to the music. It's such a vibe! I'm having the time of my life. I even began dancing with Lucie at one point! Care passes me drinks, and I down them. Then we repeat. I'm not quite sure how many I've had to be honest. I feel great! Luc doesn't look thrilled, though. I wish he would join in on the fun!

"SHOTS!" Care screams. I follow her voice and rush over. I jump into Care's arms, and sway to the music.

"Let's race! First to down the shot wins?"

"You're on! Lucie, GET OVER HERE! SHOT RACE!" Wow, Care's voice echoes. Hurriedly, Lucie rushes over. Care passes us our shots, and we prepare...

"On three...." We all eye each other. Staring intensely. "One..."
Drum roll, please. "Two..." "THREE" With that, we all gulp
down our shots. In seconds I slam my glass down on the
counter. It burns! Why does it burn? That was fun! I'm so
gonna do that again. Did I win? I think I won.

"Who won?" Lucie asks. I would like to know the same thing!

"Well, how am I meant to know! You're meant to shout when
you finish. Nobody did that. Guess we all win!" We all laugh
together. This is very fun. Well, it's very fun until I start getting
dragged somewhere by someone.

It's Luc! Yay Luc! "Luc, I've missed you!" I throw my arms
around Luc's neck. He pulls me in by my waist, Luc gives good
hugs.

"Yes, I've missed you too! This, however, is not you. You're
drunk, Ambre. We should go home and sober you up."

"Erm, I think not. I'm having so much fun! And I'm not
drunk!"

"Ambre, I'm not trying to ruin your fun. I'm just worried about
you. Please be careful, and don't overdo it. I'm staying sober all
night, so I'll keep an eye on you, come to me for anything, okay."
Aw, he cares so much, cute.

"Merci, Luc. I'm all good, though. Okay, bye!" I strut back over to the girls, and we proceed to dance ourselves to death.

My whole body aches. Why does my body ache? I'm tired. I think I should sleep, but I want to keep dancing! Dancing beats sleep. I keep dancing.

"Oh. My. God! Guys, I have an idea! Let's all do karaoke!!!" I think that's a splendid idea.

We rush through to the front room and steal the tv away from the boys, who are playing video games.

"Sorry boys, it's our turn now. Bye!" Care informs them. They do not look pleased about it. Leaving the room, they all curse us under their breaths. Ugh.

Care switches the tv over, and she selects one of the best songs ever! Stay by Rihanna. Who doesn't love that song?

All the girlies and surprisingly quite a few boys surround us and watch, dancing. First, Care, Lucie, and I, twirl each other around like princesses. Then, we all join the chorus and sing our little hearts out. My opinion? We sound *fantastic.*

I think this dance routine needs some spicing up... I make my way over to the table, stand on it and begin dancing and twirling around; I feel like a pop star! I run my hands up my body, then swish my hair back; I drop to my knees whilst still singing and looking classy the whole time, I hope.

This gets me a few howls from the boys, some whoops from the girls, a few glares from the girls who came with company, and a disappointed yet heated look from Luc. I'm too drunk for this. I look around the room, trying to find Luc's gaze again, yet I can't find him; I can't see him. That's probably because the room is spinning, and I feel very dizzy.

Wow, the lights are blurry; I don't feel good. Am I dying? Oh my God, is this what death feels like?

I attempt to pick myself back up, but I fall over my feet; I'm wearing heels. The last thing I see is the floor, coming closer and closer to my face...

Luc

The table is swarmed with boys and some extremely drunk girls. Ambre reacts well to the attention, unlike sober Ambre would. She's not sober enough to realise this isn't good attention; they're just disgusting pervs. I swear to God, if any of them so much as *try* to put their hands on her, I'll kill them. I hate that they all watch her like she's theirs for entertainment. That's *my* girl up there; those guys can get any ideas they have out of their heads.

Ambre's losing balance; she's clumsy as it is, never mind wearing heels whilst dancing on a table. I need to get her down. Just as I go to grab her, she wobbles... and then catches her feel on the corner of the table. I feel my whole body tense rushing over to catch her. I'm just praying I catch her before she hits the floor.

Ambre squeals and firmly falls into my arms; I *caught her.*

I carry her bridal style up to a bedroom, one that isn't occupied by people making out. After three awkward encounters, I find an empty room with walls covered with books. Perfect for Ambre, when she wakes up anyway.

Once Ambre wakes up, I'm hoping to sober her up a little, and convince her to go home, so she can sleep this off. However, Ambre is quite the stubborn one. And pushy, she will try to get her way. And it always works because I can't say no to that girl.

Damn you, Ambre de Roselle.

I run downstairs to grab a glass of water and a few slices of pizza for Ambs when she wakes up. If I want any chance of her saying yes to leaving, she needs to be sober.

Ambre begins to wake up. It's only been a half-hour, so she hasn't missed much of this "gathering".

She groans and lifts herself up, "Where am I? I swear I was just dancing." Ambre questions, more to herself than me.

"Morning, princess. Sleep well?"

Ambre rolls her eyes.

"You were being entertainment for the drunk boys. They seemed to find you very interesting. *Never* do that again. Unless you want someone to end up dead." It was so hard not to hit every single one of them for just looking at her that way.

"And why the hell not? I'll do what I want. Jesus, how drunk was I? My head is pounding." Did I mention she's stubborn?

"Very. You were very drunk. And yes, I know. Whatever I say doesn't even matter-" I get cut off by little miss moody over here.

"Obviously."

"Would you let me finish? Anyway, I know what I say doesn't matter. However, just think for a second. When have I ever stopped you from doing something that made you smile unless it was for a bloody good reason?"

Ambre doesn't seem to appreciate that I'm right. "Never." She Mumbles.

"Exactly. Just trust me. Okay? If you want to dance, maybe try dancing on the floor. Like normal people. Or come spin around me; I'll keep you safe, away from the pervy boys staring at you."

"Luc, were you jealous? Jealous that I was getting male attention, and it wasn't coming from you? Hm?" This girl, she's a pain.

"No, not jealous. I just didn't enjoy that they were gawking at you like you were a piece of meat. They were gaping at you as if you were *theirs*, there for their *entertainment*. And you're not. If anything, you're mine." That didn't sound so good.

"I'm yours, am I?" She taunts.

"You know what I mean; we've always been each other's, right?"

"Yes, we've always been each other's *best friend*. And we'll always stick by each other."

"Yeah, that's what I mean. Anyway, I'm protective of you. And I was so close to punching some people in the face."

Ambre laughs. "Okay, okay. Point proven. I won't dance on the tables. Nevertheless, you, Luc Bonet, were indeed jealous. Admit it." I blow out a heavy breath and laugh. She's not going to let this go, is she?

"Not jealous. You can shut up right now."

"Yeah? Make me then," She remarks. She wants to play this game? It's on.

"Are you sober?" I question. I'm not playing this game unless I know for sure she's sober.

"Unfortunately, yes. Maybe if I were still drunk it wouldn't feel like fireworks were going off inside my head."

That's everything I needed to know.

I push Ambre's shoulders back gently, causing her to lie back against the headboard. I lean over Ambre's body, one arm above her, leaning against the top of the bed frame. If I'm not mistaken, I believe I see a faint blush coat her cheeks. Ambre de Roselle, are you nervous? All her confidence from a second ago has disappeared.

We stare intently into one another's eyes. The way she looks up at me. It makes me feel some type of way. And I don't like it. I move my hand across her cheek, brushing the loose locks behind her ears. For a brief second, I swear I catch sight of Ambre's eyes lingering on my lips. The thought brings my eyes down to her lips. Her lips look soft, tender, and kissable. The opposite of how I should be seeing my best friend's lips.

We're so close. I can feel her heavy breaths against my lips. I look back into her eyes, pleading. The look on her face tells me everything I need to know. With my free hand, I lift Ambre's chin, bringing her closer to me. To my dismay, Ambre doesn't protest.

You know what? Screw it. I begin to close the distance between us, I can nearly feel her lips on mine, and this feels right. I don't care who says it's wrong. Until the door gets barged open...

"OH MY GOSH, I am so sorry. I didn't mean to interrupt. Carry on, please. But if you can, make it quick. Because we're about to play truth or dare downstairs. Okay, bye!" *Caroline.* Why does she have to have the worst timing in the world? And I could bet on anything we're not getting that chance again. Ambre shifts uncomfortably underneath me, and that's when I realise I'm still hovering over her. I move off her and sit on the other side of the bed. As far away from Ambre as possible. Now we're not touching at all. Well, this is just great, isn't it? I tried to kiss my best friend, failed, and now we have to live with this awkwardness. A redness coats Ambre's face, and she's messing with the hem of her dress. Now I've made her uncomfortable.

"Ambs, I'm sorry. I shouldn't have tried to do that."

"Luc, don't apologise. I should have stopped you, and I didn't."

"It just seemed like that's what was meant to happen, you know? I still shouldn't have done it, though."

"Luc, please just stop blaming yourself. It was weird, but it was just the timing. We both made a mistake. Let's not make it again, and we can just move on from this." *A mistake?* Right, okay.

"Yeah, let's go downstairs. Caroline wanted us anyway." She gives me a flat smile and hurries past me. She's cautious not to brush me on the way out. I can't believe this happened. I thought something was really about to happen. All I know is that I can't lose Ambre to some silly mistake, awkward or not; I need this girl.

It's now eleven pm. Most people have gone home now. There are about ten of us here now. A few randoms, I don't know. And then the "group", I suppose. They've been calling us that anyway; Ambre, Lucie, Caroline, Alexandre, and I. I've been told to call him Alex, but I think I'll stick to Alexandre just to annoy him. Annoying people is a *fantastic* way to make friends. *Not.* However, I'm not looking to exactly be "bros" with Alex. So if I call him Alexandre, he'll dislike me, and I won't have someone trying to befriend me or talk to me. Simple.

We all sit in a circle on the floor. We look like high school kids about to play spin the bottle. It's ridiculous. Ambre and Caroline sit across from Lucie and I. Alex is also sitting beside Ambre. Which exasperates me. I already dislike Alex. I won't say hate; hate is strong. There are many people I strongly dislike. Only a few people I hate.

Since the incident upstairs, Ambre is refusing to even look my way. She hasn't said a word to me. I can't deal with this.

Awkwardness isn't a pleasant feeling with anyone; now imagine it with your best friend.

Caroline interrupts my train of thought when she gets the game started. "Okay! Let's start. Ambre first! Then we can go around in a circle. Ambre, truth or dare?"

Ambre, please don't pick dare. This is Caroline. God knows what she'll make her do.

"Dare." Great. Just great.

"I dare you to send a flirty message to the person you find hottest in the room. Everyone, turn your volume up!"

Caroline looks over at me and mouths, "I got you!" Oh. She's assuming Ambre will message me because of what she walked in on. The room goes silent. Everyone looks around, trying to find out who Ambre's messaged. I'd like to know the same thing. I hear a ping... from across the room. And see a very pleased Alex, smirking down at his phone. *Ouch.* I should've known she wouldn't message me. But I still had a bit of hope. Caroline looks shocked.

"Care to share the message, Alex?" Caroline asks him, nosey as always.

"Nah, I think I'll keep this one to myself," He says, winking at Ambre with a smug look.

"Okay! Who's next?"

We go around in a circle until it's finally my turn. I'm dreading this. But I'm showing Ambre that she hasn't fazed me. I'll choose dare.

"Luc, truth or dare?" Caroline questions.

"Dare." Here we go.

"I dare you to kiss the hottest person in this room." Crap. Okay, I've got two options here. I can make Ambre jealous by kissing Lucie, or I could... You know what? I'll make her regret choosing Alex. I'll show her who's hot.

I hesitantly stand. Making my way over to her, I'm ready. Hell, I've been ready for this my entire life. I extend my hand, pulling her to stand with me. I stare intently into her deep blue eyes; she looks anxious, *almost* excited. I gently stroke her face, trailing my fingers over the freckles scattered across her nose. I brush her curls behind her ears. *Deja vu.* This reminds me of our *almost* kiss before.

There's so much tension standing between us right now. My heart beats rapidly against Ambre's chest. No doubt she can feel how nervous I am. I need her more than I've needed anything in my life. I place my hand on the back of her head to bring her closer to me. I search Ambre's eyes for approval, and she again doesn't protest.

I press my lips firmly to hers.

I'm kissing Ambre. I'm kissing my best friend. All I can think of at this moment is, why haven't we been doing this our whole lives? Her lips fit with mine like they were made for each other. Pulling her closer, I deepen the kiss. Kissing her like the world is about to end. For a moment, I let myself forget that we're in a room full of people. Because I know, once this kiss stops, it doesn't just stop temporarily. This isn't 'to be continued'. Because we're Ambre and Luc. *Friends.* Not lovers.

Ambre pulls away, breaking the kiss. I stare down at her. Both of us breathe heavily. I search her face for something, anything that lets me know that what I just did was okay. Even though we both know it wasn't. I hate myself for what I just did.

I hate myself even more because I loved every second of it.

I'd jump at the chance to do it again. Again, again, and again. Her face tells me nothing other than the fact that I screwed up. I'd be happier if she were mad. Ambre's not angry; she's sad. Her eyes become slightly glossy. She won't even look at me. I hate seeing *my Ambre* this way. Anyone who's caused her upset in the past has always regretted it. I'd always deal with them. Except now, it's me. *I'm* the one who made her feel this way. What is wrong with me?

Ambre

What the actual hell just happened? I don't know how to react. I should not have enjoyed that as much as I did. However, this isn't right. Luc is my best friend. Has been my whole life. I'm pretty much the only person he has left. He's my person. I can't imagine life without him. And I'm sure he doesn't want to lose me either. Hey, *sometimes* these things work out. But what if it didn't? What if things got messy? As soon as we let things go over the line, it ruins our friendship. Our friendship of near enough eighteen years.

I already know things are going to get messy now. He can use the excuse 'it was a dare' all he likes. He didn't have to choose me. Caroline said to kiss the hottest person in the room. Lucie is sitting right next to him. What have you done, Luc?

"Well, that got pretty heated!" Care says with a light-hearted giggle. Surely she's just trying to lift the mood a bit. "Anyways, let's carry on with the game."

I need to get out of here. But if I leave now, they'll all know how much it fazed me. I can't let them see that despite how nauseous I currently feel.

"Lucie, truth or dare."

"Well, we've already had two pretty heated dares," She laughs. She seems almost as uneasy as me. "So truth. I guess."

"Okay, if you could have a makeout sesh with anyone in this room, who would it be, and why?" Oh, God.

"Well, that's a confusing one. You see, I would have made out with Luc, no doubt. However, as we all saw, he just did that with Ambre." Uh-oh.

"Nothing is going on, Lucie. Luc and I, we're just friends. And we'll only ever be friends. So he's all yours." I can't bare to look at Luc's face. He looked distraught when I said that, but only for a split second. Then as Luc does, he puts up a front.

"You might want to tell yourself that. You seemed pretty into him two seconds ago. You know when you were standing there snogging in front of a group of people?" Damn you, Luc Bonet.

"Lucie, I can tell you like him," It feels awkward having this conversation in front of loads of people. But here we are. "I will prove to you that I have no feelings for Luc." How will I do that? I have no flipping idea.

"I don't believe that for a second. But feel free."

I can't believe I'm about to do this after Luc just kissed me. For his sake, I hope he leaves. Alex sitting to my right, is currently clueless, sitting back, most probably entertained by all of this. If I'm going to do this, I might as well make a show out of it.

I slide onto his lap and pull him close to me from behind his neck. I stare at his lips for a second. Debating whether or not I should do this. If I overthink, I'll talk myself out of it. Without warning, I crash my lips onto his. Pulling back, I give him a wry smile.

I feel guilty. I used Alex to prove I don't have feelings for Luc. *Now I'm trying to prove that to myself as well.*

⚐ *Chapter 6* ⚐

Ambre

I woke up this morning feeling dreadful. The hangover didn't help the matter. Okay, so maybe I got a *little* drunk. That's my excuse for everything I did last night anyway.

Perhaps I could tell Luc that I remember nothing? It would save me the awkwardness for sure. But, having said that, I can't save Luc from the pain I caused him.

I would have moved past that first incident thinking it was just the heat of the moment and we'd both had too much to drink. But now I'm thinking back, Luc didn't drink a single drop of alcohol.

Then Luc kissed me. *He actually kissed me.* Not even just a peck. That was a kiss kiss. The worst part is, I can't say I hated it.

Despite how much I may or may not have enjoyed it, I know that Luc will *only* ever be a friend. Plus, my feelings for him will always remain platonic. No matter what.

I mean, I can now say that my best friend is a good kisser, a *really* good kisser.

We're now going to forget the incidents of yesterday! Well, I'm going to try. I can't speak for Luc. His heart is likely aching a lot more than mine. It only hurt me because Luc's my person. I need him.

Then, with him kissing me, things got awkward. I don't recall the last time things were awkward between Luc and I. We have flirty banter, sure. But, still, that's all harmless.

Now from Luc's perspective, he kissed me. I told another girl she could have him, then made out with Alex. So if Luc hates me, I don't blame him.

I went to English lit this morning. I'm now at the cafe, except no Luc is to be seen. I knew kissing Alex was a bad idea.

I should have just let Lucie think whatever the hell she wants. I could have confronted Luc in private. We could've been okay. This is all my fault. I'm confused, I'm tired, and I miss Luc.

Luc

I left an hour earlier than usual today for obvious reasons. To be completely honest, I have no clue what to do. This is such a bizarre thing for Ambre and me; we're usually inseparable.

Do I apologise? Does she apologise? I mean, I guess she doesn't really have a reason to apologise. Ambre can kiss whoever the hell she wants. Who am I to stand in the way?

It hurt. Hearing her say those things to Lucie right after, I put myself out there for her, right in front of my face. Then to go kiss Alex as well? That's just a bit harsh. Like, come on, at least wait for me to leave.

I take full responsibility for our kiss. I shouldn't have done it, she's Ambre: *my best friend*. Not some random girl I can just kiss. I don't know what came over me. We were messing about, playfully flirting as we always do. I moved over to her, looked down at her; she looked breathtaking. Her lips were just begging to be kissed. So, I tried to kiss her. Until we were interrupted, so I took the next opportunity I got; the dare. And I loved it. I won't even lie; it was pretty amazing. Apparently, I'm the only one who thought so.

Where do we go from here, then? I suppose it's safe to say I may like Ambre a little more than a friend...

But how I feel about her doesn't matter. I already know how she feels. I don't want to push her. If she liked me, she'd tell me. I have to trust that.

But what do I do for the rest of my life after this? Sit back and watch Ambre and Alex ride off into the sunset? I think the hell not. I need to do something, anything.

Maybe a little convincing? I'll charm her. I'll show her what it feels like to be flirted with by Luc Bonet. I don't flirt with people often, but when I do, *I do it well.* And, if she tells me to just bugger off at any point, I will.

So, as it turns out, I don't know how to flirt with my best friend. Ironic, as all we do, is flirt. To be fair, though, that was all harmless banter. Now I'm *actually* trying to flirt with her. Which is probably the worst idea I've ever had in my life. One, she's my longest and only friend, two, I have a hunch she *may* be interested in Alex. After snogging him in front of me and all.

I don't know the best way to go around this. We need to break this ice. We haven't spoken much, and it's driving me mad.

I'm turning to my last resort. I'm calling bloody Caroline.

"This is a peculiar experience. Luc, are you dying? Why on earth are you calling me?"

"This is serious; I need help wi-" I get cut off by Caroline shouting in the background.

"For the love of God, shut up, Beau! Nobody cares what *your* snarky mouth has to say." I can almost see the eye roll. "Sorry, Luc, continue."

"As I was saying," I add more firmly, "I need help with Ambre. We haven't spoken, and she won't so much as look my way."

"Honestly, I'm hyped that you guys kissed. At least you were bold enough to make the first move. She'll come around. She's just scared, and that's understandable." I suppose she's right there.

"What do I do from here, though? It's too awkward."

"You're the best friend, Luc, well, the OG best friend. Of course, I'm her best friend now," She says more to herself.

"Caroline! Stop getting sidetracked."

"Hush, loverboy. If you want my help, you don't get shouty with me. Got it?"

"Got it." I Mumble.

"First, you need to be the one to get rid of the initial awkwardness. Get her something she loves, to make conversation. "

"Thank you, Caroline. You were actually helpful for once."

"You're welcome! And just you remember this next time you make some sarcastic comment towards me."

"Yeah yeah. Bye, Caroline."

That was somewhat of a success. I'm going to find a limited edition version of Ambre's favourite book. One she's been looking for, for years. They don't sell anymore; they don't get printed anymore. I'm pretty sure they're illegal to sell them anymore because they were a one-time thing.

But I have connections. And I'm calling in my long-overdue favour.

He picks up on the second ring.

"Luc Bonet. I wasn't sure if I'd ever hear from you."

"I'm calling in my favour."

"Tell me what you need. I'll sort it out. But after this, you forget everything that happened; I owe you nothing. Eric owes you nothing. Got it?"

"I know how it works. If you can get me what I want, I'll forget it ever happened. Erase it from my mind." I wish I could erase it from my mind. Those memories are what keep me up at night.

"Good. Now, what do you want? Do we need to discuss this in person?"

"No. I want you to get me a certain book. I'll send you a picture."

"That's all? I offered to kill a man if you needed me to, and you want a bloody book? God, you're stupid. Send it, and it's done. I'll have it for you by tonight."

I don't bother replying. I just hung up. I won't listen to that man's voice any longer than I have to.

That was Daniel Maxwell, aka the biggest CEO in London. Aka, Eric's brother.

⚑

The sun's setting. I'm standing out on the balcony. Admiring the sky. Daniel got that book to me like he said he would. It doesn't surprise me that he got it. As he said, he could kill someone if he wanted to.

You know, I've never felt at home anywhere. No *place* anyway. I suppose home for me has always been Ambre. So long as she's with me, I'm home. Now we're together, and in Paris, wow. It's perfect.

Apart from the fact that this beautiful place also comes with people. People who either want to replace my role of best friend or become the role of the boyfriend.

The door opens ever so quietly. As if she's trying her very hardest to keep quiet. Keep from attracting my attention.

Not happening. She can try to avoid this all she wants. We're
not leaving it.

"Ambre." She looks like a teenager who's just been caught
sneaking in after a night out.

"Luc." To my surprise, she makes her way over to stand on the
balcony with me. I hold fire on giving her the book just yet. I
don't want her to feel like she *has* to speak to me just because I
got her something.

"Ambre, I hate this. The tension. Look, I know I shouldn't have
kissed you. *I know.* But I'm not going to apologise for something
that felt right."

"Luc, I'm not saying it didn't feel right. But we're friends. You
have to know it won't work, right?" Ouch.

"It could work if we made it." I stare into her eyes, pleading.

"How? Because when I see us as a couple, I see us losing our
friendship. I see us becoming every couple in this world:
Fighting, shouting, arguing, losing love. Except we wouldn't just
be losing love, would we? We'd be losing our friendship, Luc."

"We're not most people. We're Ambre and Luc. We make things
work. And we get through it. There have been times when I've
thought, how the hell did I survive that? It's because I had you.
Because I've always had you,"

"Luc, I- " She's lost for words. "I don't know what to say."

"Say okay. Say you trust me. Say we can make this work." I plead.

"I *can't*. It's not that easy, and you know it." Her eyes begin to go glossy.

"Why? Why can't it be that easy."

"Because I don't even know how I feel! This is all so sudden! First, there was that blip in the bedroom-"

"A blip? That's what you want to call it?"

"Yes, Luc. It was a freaking blip. It shouldn't have happened, and you know it. We were messing around, and we let it get way too heated. Then there was truth or dare. And can I just ask, why me? Lucie, who is absolutely breathtaking, sat right next to you. Why not kiss her?"

"Because Ambre. *She's not you.* I didn't want to kiss Lucie. I wanted to kiss you. I really wanted to kiss you. And you know what? I don't regret it because it was hot and passionate, and it was a damn good kiss. You can try to say you didn't enjoy it, but I-"

"I *did* enjoy it! God, Luc, shut up. Yes, okay. It was so freaking hot. I loved the way your lips felt against mine. You're an amazing kisser, and as much as I want to say I hated it, I didn't. I wish we could do it every single day for the rest of our lives. But that doesn't change anything! We have chemistry. But that doesn't mean I want to risk our friendship, just for some mind-blowing kisses."

Mind-Blowing kisses? I look down, smirking. I try to hide it; honestly, I do. I know this isn't the right time. But she just admitted that she loved it as much as I did. It wasn't just me. Then why did she feel the need to kiss Alex? Why would she tell Lucie she can have me if she felt the same way I did?

"Why did you kiss Alexandre?"

"I needed to show Lucie that I'm not into *you*. So I kissed *him*."

"So you're definitely not into me? Because after the way you just described our kiss, it sounds like you might be into me."

"Luc, I don't know. I'm confused. I love you as my best friend; it's hard to separate those feelings."

"But you did enjoy the kiss?"

"Yes, I enjoyed the kiss. I don't see how that has anything to do with this, though."

"Just checking before I do this." I feel like this probably isn't the best thing to do at this moment. But Ambre needs a slight swaying.

I pull Ambre in by her waist, her hair in a messy bun tied with a purple ribbon today.

I stoke the sides of her face. Her cheeks are blush pink. The sun caught her face. It's adorable. Her eyes search mine and briefly dip down to my lips. She hesitantly moves her hands up to my chest; I momentarily expect her to shove me away. She doesn't. Instead, she moves her hands down to the hem of my t-shirt, getting more confident. She slowly runs her hands up my chest, sending sparks through my entire body. This girl is going to kill me. And I love her for it.

I need to make sure she still wants to kiss me; the last thing I want is for her to feel uncomfortable right now. "If you tell me to stop and walk away right now, I will."

"We both know that's not going to happen, Luc."

With that, she brings one of her hands to the back of my neck, leaving the other one to rest against my chest. She pulls my face down to hers. Smirking, I look down at her lips before kissing her.

"You're ridiculously attractive, princess."

"Shut up and kiss me, Bonet." Bonet? She means business. Best not keep the princess waiting. I press my lips to hers, kissing her passionately. I pull her closer by her waist, deepening the kiss. I feel her warm breath against mine. She must be enjoying this as much as I. For a while, we just stay in the moment. Kissing like it's the last time.

If we were in a movie, this would be the moment when fireworks would go off. I mean, this might actually be better. Sunset, Eiffel tower standing tall behind us. The smell of croissants in the bakery across from us.

Nothing could make this moment better except if Ambre told me that she was choosing to say yes to us. But that's not happening. So for now, I'll stay here. In this moment, pretending like it might not be the last time we get to do this.

A Chapter 7 A

Ambre

I don't even know what just happened. One minute we were arguing, then we were kissing. Now, I'm even more confused than ever. All I know is that I really, really enjoy kissing Luc. Which is wrong. He's my best friend. I can't think of him this way. What should I do? I suppose Luc made a few valid points during our argument.

We're not most people. We're Ambre and Luc. We make everything work.

He was right there; we do make everything work.

Honestly, I'm scared. This entire journey has been challenging. The moving city. The being away from Ami every day. Sleeping alone every night without my cat to keep me company. I miss it all so freaking much. But I've survived it. And Luc is the reason for that.

Maybe we could work. Although all of this means we *might* be able to work as a couple, I don't even know if I want that. Sure he's a good kisser, and he takes care of me, and he's just all-around amazing, but despite all of that, he's still Luc; my best friend. Not my boyfriend. I don't think that can change. At least not for a while, I'm not ready.

A soft knock at my door tears me away from my thought bubble.

"Come in," I say hesitantly. I don't know if I'm ready to face him after my conclusion.

"Morning princess. How's the re-read going?"

Once Luc and I had finished kissing last night, he sat me down and gave me a limited edition of my favourite book. How he got his hands on that, I don't know. I was astonished, and I still am. I appreciate it so freaking much, but I'm worried that it was some sort of grand gesture to try to win me over. How am I meant to tell him that I don't want to be with him now?

"It's going great. Thank you again. You really shouldn't have gone to the trouble. You're an amazing *friend*, Luc."

I'm sorry, I'm sorry, I'm sorry.

I see Luc's face drop for a second until he hides it. Luc's always been good at hiding his feelings, so it's always been a pain for me to read him.

"You're welcome. Don't worry about it. A special book for a special girl." He gives me a half-smile.

He knows my demeanour has changed since last night. I can see it in his eyes. Luc is great at hiding his emotions. However, his eyes show everything. That is something he'll never be able to hide. That's the only way I can read him when he doesn't feel like opening up.

"Luc, we need to talk about last night," I say, defeated.

"Don't bother Ambre. I already know what you're going to say."

"I'm sorry."

"See, you say that, but I don't understand how you can be sorry but be giving me these mixed signals."

"When have I ever given mixed signals? I have always been completely honest about my feelings towards you, Luc."

"That time where we *almost* kissed, it was me initiating it. But you're not entirely innocent either. You were flirting with me, you made me think for a second that you might actually have some type of feelings for me-" Is he bringing this up? I can't believe him.

"Luc, I told you straight after that it was a mistake! Then you kissed me after I made it clear we shouldn't do it again."

"I didn't force you to kiss me; we could ask anyone in that room. Even bloody Lucie said *you* seemed into it. Try getting yourself out of that one, princess." He looks so smug, like he caught me out. He hasn't.

"I kissed you because *it was a dare*. I didn't want to make a scene in a room full of people! And for the love of God, stop calling me princess! I am *not* your princess. And I never will be!"

And he carries on. "Not to mention last night, I told you to tell me to stop if you wanted to. I believe your words were 'that's not going to happen' Then *you* pulled *me* in. And now here we are. You're *yet again* turning me away."

"You'd think after being turned away so many times, you'd get the hint." I spit out.

"You know what? I don't like this Ambre. What's happened to my sweet Ambre, hm? Who would never intentionally hurt people around her. Because you sure as hell aren't her. "

"Luc, I'm-"

He cuts me off. "I don't care what you are. Come speak to me when *my Ambre* has come back." He says, full of spite.

"I'm still here, Luc. I'm the same Ambre. The only difference is that I've gotten fed up with telling you *no*. We wouldn't be here if you hadn't kissed me that first night."

"Stop digging yourself a hole, Ambre. Just leave me the hell alone from now on."

Luc

Ambre's words hurt me. They really hurt me.

'I'm not your princess, and I never will be.'

There wasn't any need for that. It was a harmless nickname. I don't understand her. Last night I was so sure we'd made progress that we were going somewhere. Then, all of a sudden, this morning, she just changed. Like she can't make up her mind. It's killing me.

The last time I felt this alone was when my Mam died. When I was left alone with Eric. I'm scared to feel that way again; I'm scared to be alone again. But it's all coming back. I can't stop it. The memories come flooding back, just like they used to when I was a kid. Harsh, quickly, all at once. Flooding my brain.

"What the bloody hell is this?" Eric came barging into my room with my grade paper.

"It's a C plus, Eric."

"Yeah, I can see that, you sarcastic brat."

"I wasn't being sarcastic, I swear!"

"Shut your mouth before I shut it for you." I winced. He wasn't lying. Eric never bluffed.

"Your parents would be so disappointed in you." Why does he always bring them up in a bad sense? It hurts me so much. My eyes

start to sting, I can't cry. He'll only hurt me more for showing
weakness.

"They always said my grades don't define me as a person, if I tried
my hardest then that's all that matters."

"Shame they're not here to wipe the pathetic tears off your face.
You're worthless. Nobody in this world loves you anymore. Nobody
will ever love you. I'm all you've got, and not even I bloody love
you. Remember that kid? Don't you come crying to me when you're
homeless, you sure as hell won't be living with me."

I sobbed as he struck me, again, again and again. Until
eventually, I didn't feel it anymore. My back was numb. My sight
was blurred with red. All I saw was darkness starting to cloud my
vision, then nothing. This time because of a grade. Last time for
crying when I missed my parents. I'm afraid of the future.

I'm in a puddle of sweat, shaking. They've come back. The
flashbacks. I'm well and truly screwed now. I've not had
flashbacks like that for years. Those feelings never came back
until now.

Those punishments made me fear every single grade I ever got. If
I didn't reach B+ at least, it would be a fearful, painful night.
That's how I got to the top of my class, how I got grades good
enough to get into this university.

Eric ruined my childhood. The abuse never stopped. Unless he had female company of course, then he was the world's greatest step-Dad.

Not until I reached the age where I was stronger, anyway I could fight back. Unless he was drunk. There was no winning if Eric was drunk, he got more aggresive, it seemed as if it was an animal-like instinct in his brain. He saw me as his prey, and he attacked.

Still, then, I never hit him as hard as I should have. I couldn't let Henry see his Dad in such a state. Nobody should see a parent that way. Eric was an awful man, but he never laid a finger on Henry. Henry didn't know what his father was capable of. It's something I pray he never knows.

Chapter 8

Ambre

For the past two weeks, I've been staying with Care. It's been different having three roommates. It's also given me the chance to get to know Alex and Lucie better, so that's a perk. They've been so welcoming; I do feel somewhat at home here.

Honestly, it's been so peculiar not being with Luc. I've entirely avoided him for weeks. I can't face him. I do feel guilty for the things I said to him. It must be confusing. But at the same time, he's hurting me by ruining our friendship.

I love Luc. Just not in the way he wants me to.

Caroline has tried countless times to get Luc and I to talk. But it's not happening. I'm not talking to him. Luc told me to stay the hell away from him. So that's what I'm doing. I suppose all friendships end eventually...even ones that have lasted nearly eighteen years.

"Hey, pretty girl. What you watching?" Alex and I have gotten a lot closer these past couple of weeks. Nothing romantic. As much as I currently resent Luc, I couldn't do that to him. Not after he admitted to having feelings for me.

"Hey, handsome," Just our nicknames. "I'm watching a romance movie. It's just started. Wanna join?"

"As if I'd turn down a movie day, even if it is a sappy romance movie." He says, jumping onto the bed.

"Hey! My sappy romance movies are quite exquisite." I say defensively.

"Oh, are they now?" He questions amusingly. I give him the side-eye and click play.

I groan and open my eyes. Did I fall asleep? You've got to be joking. I *love* that film. This will not help my case about my romance films being exquisite.

"Morning, pretty girl. Sleep well?"

I now realise that not only did I fall asleep. I fell asleep with Alex, and I'm currently cuddled up to him.

And it feels... *nice?*

"I didn't mean to fall asleep; I must've been exhausted."

"I could tell. You started shivering, so I put a blanket over us. Hope you don't mind. Also, you snore, you know?" How freaking embarrassing.

"You don't mention that to anyone, got it?"

"My lips are sealed." He winks. And I feel my stomach flip. *Oh, God. Oh, God. Oh, God.*

I can *not* have a crush on my roommate. I live here. Imagine how awkward it would be if I *liked* him.

"You okay there, Ambs? You look like you're contemplating life." *I am.*

That's when someone opens the door.

"Oh my God. I'm sorry for interrupting." Lucie says as she covers her eyes, backing out of the room.

"Alex?" I ask cautiously.

"Yep. We're screwed." He sounds just as panicked as I feel.

Luc

Living in *our* apartment alone has been hell. Every morning I wake up expecting to hear the shower running; I look forward to hearing her soft singing.

It feels as if I'm grieving a friendship. And that can't be the case. Our friendship can't be a lost cause. It just can't.

As much as Ambre's been driving me insane with these mixed signals, she's still my best friend. I just wish she were more.

A knock on the door takes me away from my bubble of thought. Who the hell would come here? All of Ambre's friends know she's not currently staying here.

What if it's Ambre?

I open the door, and...Lucie comes rushing through. Well, this is normal.

"Everything okay? Ambre's not here. You know that, right?"

"Yes, obviously I know that. She's living in *my* home. This is about Ambre. There's something you should know."

What the hell. I'm internally freaking the hell out. Is she hurt? Has something bad happened to her?

"What? Lucie spit it out."

"So, I know you two are a bit complicated right now. And I know that you have feelings for her. I just don't know what exactly you are. A situationship? I don't know," She Mumbles on. Speaking more to herself.

"Lucie! Will you stop rambling and tell me what the hell is wrong with Ambre."

"Oh no, nothing's wrong with her, don't worry about that." I feel so relieved.

"Okay, what is it then? I don't have all day."

"I walked into her room before, and she was lying in bed with Alex. They were under a blanket." I'm going to kill him.

"Please tell me this is some cruel joke, Lucie."

She looks down. "I'm sorry."

My head spins. She made it clear she didn't want anything to do with me but to go off, and I don't even know what they were doing. Sleeping together? Cuddling? Making out? It hurts. I thought I meant more to her than that.

Ambre doesn't feel *anything* for me. Not even as friends, apparently. Friends don't hurt friends.

"Luc, are you okay?"

"I'm great. Just flipping great."

"I can't even begin to imagine how betrayed you must feel right now. But Luc, you can't let her get to you."

"Lucie, I don't want your sympathy."

There's nothing worse than having people look at you like you're some helpless puppy. Someone who needs to be saved. I'd sooner die than take somebody's sympathy.

"This isn't sympathy, Luc. I think we both need a friend right now."

"Why? What's wrong with you?"

"Honestly, this sounds so petty and childish,"

"I don't judge."

"It's been hard adjusting to having Ambre live with us and be a part of our little group. She and Caroline are so close now that I feel almost abandoned. I know Care still loves me, but all I can think about is, what if she loves Ambre more? And before you came along, I had a slight crush on Alex. *Clearly* he likes *her*."

"Sorry, go back to that last sentence quickly. Before I came along? What do you mean by that?"

"As I made clear in truth or dare, I like you, Luc. I don't know you very well, but I'd really like to."

"Stay here." I don't know what drove me to say that. But you know what? I don't even regret it.

Screw you, Ambre de Roselle.

"*What?*"

"Stay here. If Ambre's making you uncomfortable, and we both need the company, stay here."

"Where would I sleep? I'm not taking Ambre's room; it'd be wrong."

"Well, I'd say take my bed, and I'll take the couch, but I'm not that much of a gentleman. So just stay with me."

"Stay with you? In your bedroom? As in, we sleep in the same bed?"

"Yes. Am I speaking Spanish?"

"No, I'm just confused. You like Ambre, but you're asking me to stay with you. In your room."

"I promise I won't go near you. You, however, might not be able to hold yourself back." I add with a wink.

She smiles. "I'm sure I'll do just fine. Okay, I'll stay with you. Wait, what if Ambre finds out? Won't she be mad?"

"Ambre doesn't have the right to be mad. She's off doing *whatever* with Alexandre. So we can do whatever the hell we'd like. Let her think what she wants."

"You're right. Okay, I'm going to head home and grab some clothes."

"You can just sleep in one of my t-shirts."

She giggles. "Thank you for that lovely offer; I'll probably take you up on that. I am, however, still going to go get some things." Then she's gone.

A pang of guilt stings my chest. I don't know why I feel guilty. Ambre doesn't like me. So it's time I get over her. *And maybe our friendship.*

Chapter 9

Luc

It's ten pm, Lucie and I are sitting in the front room watching a
movie. I'm actually quite enjoying her company. It's not often I
enjoy anyone's company except Ambre's, of course.

This is nice.

Lucie visibly shivers on the other end of the couch. "Luc, why
the heck are your windows open? It's bloody freezing!"

"What are you on about? It's warm if anything."

"I'm freezing!"

"Go put some clothes on then! You *are* in tiny shorts and a crop
top."

"I'm comfy."

"Fine. Come here" I open my arms to her.

This is so unlike me. First, letting a random girl stay with me,
then let her share my bed, and now I'm offering to cuddle her.
Ambre has got me messed up.

"You're offering to cuddle me?"

"Yes. Now get over here before I change my mind." She scoots over to me, and we both lie across the couch. She rests her head against my chest while I put my arms around her waist.

"You're so warm, Luc."

"Yes, because it's not cold in here!"

"Oh, shush."

Ten minutes into the film, Lucie is flat-out. I suppose it's bedtime, then.

Carefully, I lift Lucie, so her legs wrap around my waist, her arms around my neck. And I carry her to bed.

After I've laid Lucie down, I strip from my top, leaving me in plaid pyjama pants. Finally, after a long, eventful day, I decide to sleep. I think this is the earliest I've slept in a while.

I'm forced to sit here listening to Eric and Daniel talk bad about my parents. And I can't say a word about it. I know what's coming if I do.

"My brother, if I'm frank, I'm glad that waste of space died. She was worthless to me. And now I'm stuck with this disappointment." He motions to me.

I can't believe the words I'm hearing. I don't think I can hold myself back if he says one more thing. For my safety, I should. But I can't.

"Nah, she was a good lay, that's all. I would've gotten rid of her sooner or later." *That was my last straw.*

"What the hell did you just say about my mother?"

"What did I say before Dan got here? I said you'll keep your goddamn mouth closed, or you'll regret it. What did you just do? Open your mouth. What are you going to do now? Regret it." *He says through clenched teeth.*

I'm so sick of this vile man. I want him gone. I want him locked up. Henry will be better off without him.

"You know what Eric? I'm so sick of you. You're a disgusting man. You don't deserve Henry or me in your life. And you sure as hell didn't deserve my mother!"

"That's it. I warned you. You're going to wish you never said a word, kid."

With that, he pulls out a pocket knife. He's not going to... is he?

His brother joins in now. "Eric, don't do something you're going to regret. If you kill him, it could ruin your life."

Kill, *I was worried that's what he was trying to do.*

Eric stomps over to me, grabs me by the collar of my shirt and slams me to the ground.

I fight, and I fight, and I fight. But Eric's drunk. And drunk Eric is even more assertive than sober Eric.

He brings his knife to my throat, he presses it down, not enough to kill me or fatally injure me, but enough to scare me. Then, with his other hand, he begins to strangle me. I can't breathe.

"After this, you'll think twice before ignoring me. Oh, wait," He adds mockingly. " there won't be a next time if you're dead." He says with a vicious smile. The smell of beer is all I can smell coming off him.

Black spots start to cover everything. My vision fades in and out. I gasp for air. I try, I try, and I try to wriggle free of his grasp. Nothing works.

I close my eyes, and I pray to Mam and Papa; I beg them to save me. I can't leave Henry alone in this world. I can't leave my Ambre.

It feels like an eternity that I've been gasping for air, fighting for my life. Until I hear a loud crash.

I can breathe again.

I open my eyes to see Daniel punching Eric.

"Get it together man! You kill that kid, and his blood is on your hands. And mine. I can't afford that. Now I've got to clean up your damn mess!"

Eric lies motionless on the floor. He just accepts the hits. He's exhausted. So he stays.

Daniel makes his way over to me. What if he finishes what Eric started? What if he's going to get rid of me for good?

"I'm sorry about that, mate." *He reaches out his hand. I take it; I don't think I could stand alone if I tried.*

"He nearly killed me. I thought I was dying."

"I know. Look, this has to stay between us."

"Are you crazy? He nearly killed me. I'm taking him to the cops. I don't want that psychopath around my brother."

"I can't let you do that. I promise Eric will never touch your brother. He'd never dream of it. I know you don't see that side of him, but he's a good Dad to Henry. He'd never let anyone lay a finger on him. He loves that kid."

"If he ever hurts my brother, I'll do something that I'll really regret. But I will do it. And that's a bloody promise."

"I don't doubt it. I'll check-in. I'll keep Henry safe. As for you, I need you to tell me right now that your lips are sealed."

"I can't do that."

"You have to do that. Tell you what, if you can promise me your silence. I'll owe you."

"You'll owe me? Like hell, you'll owe me. You already owe me for your brother trying to kill me!"

"You're not listening to me! I will owe you. When I owe somebody, I do what they want to be done, no questions asked. Do you want somebody dead? Done. You want something illegal, not found anywhere in this world? Done."

"How do I know I can trust you?"

"You don't. You just have to put your trust in me. I saved your life, didn't I?"

"Fine. You have yourself a deal. I'll keep quiet."

I wake up gasping for air. I've tried so damn hard to erase that memory from my mind. A tear slips down my cheek. That was the most terrifying thing that's ever happened to me. I thought I was as good as dead.

It happened last year. I was sixteen.

"Luc? Luc, are you okay? You're shaking. What's going on?" She sounds genuinely worried. She cares.

"It doesn't matter."

"Luc, it matters. I've never seen you like this."

"And you won't again."

"What happened? Bad dream?"

"Just a vile flashback. I'm fine now."

"No, you're not. And that's okay." She pulls me to lie in her lap. I've never felt so safe with someone so quickly. Lucie gets me.

She's comforting; I wouldn't mind her sticking around for a while.

I cuddle into her, letting myself feel for a second. Eric messed me up. As much as I try to forget everything, leave him in my past, he's still there, in my memories. He stays there taunting me.

I sit back up. "Thanks, Lucie. I appreciate you being there for me. Feel free to stay for as long as you want."

"I might just take you up on that offer." She adds with a smile. Her smile really is beautiful.

"Hey, Lucie?"

"Yes?"

"I'm probably going to regret asking you this. My head is everywhere, so it's probably not the smartest thing for me to ask for right now. I'm stupidly missing Ambre, you've made me feel safer than I have in a while, and you're crazy hot,"

"Luc, where are you going with this?"

I look down at her lips. She notices. She looks down at mine.

"Can I kiss you?"

"Luc, you don't know how long I've waited for you to ask me that."

"So, yes?"

"Obviously!"

I smirk and pull her to sit on my lap. She sits facing me.

"How have I never noticed how bloody hot you are?"

She goes visibly red. "I've been waiting for you to realise." She adds jokingly.

I place my hand on the back of her head and pull her in, and then I crush my lips onto hers.

Lucie is a phenomenal kisser. She really is.

Almost as good as Ambre. My brain just has to throw in there. Great. I am so very screwed.

Chapter 10

Ambre

"Hey, pretty girl. Fancy going on a little picnic date?" Alex says, walking into the living room where I'm reading.

"Well, hello there, handsome. Is this you officially asking me on a date?"

"I suppose it is."

"Hmm, I might have to think about my answer for a little while," I say jokingly.

Alex walks up to me and swoops me into his arms, bridal style.

"Alex put me down!" I say laughing.

"So, how about that date," He says, staring into my eyes.

"Okay, okay, fine, if you put me down." I agree as he places me on the couch.

"You're crazy."

"Crazy about you." He says dramatically, winking.

"You don't know me enough to be crazy about me. Sorry to break it to you, handsome."

"Well, what do you think this date is for? Hm, pretty girl?"

"Fine, point made. I'll go on a date with you."

"Perfect. See you in an hour. I'll be waiting." He says all smiley.

I walk down the stairs in a lilac, knee-length, flowy dress. It's my favourite summer dress. And I see Alex waiting for me at the bottom, wearing a navy blue t-shirt, and faded grey jeans. He does look rather handsome, I must say. The navy top matches his ocean-like eyes.

"Beautiful girl." He says, looking me up and down as I reach the bottom of the stairs. The feeling I get in my stomach as he does this startles me.

"What happened to pretty girl?"

"You, Ambre, are just too beautiful to be called anything else."

"You're such a sweet talker, Alex."

"Only for you, beautiful." I smile at my feet. I'm not sure if I like the effect he's having on me.

"Give me a twirl then." He says, exchanging his hand.

As I take his hand, he twirls me around, catching me in his arms as he dips me.

We don't move for a good *long* five seconds, I stare at him, and he stares back. My eyes dip to his lips. *I know what those lips feel like.* The memory brings an unwanted flush to my cheeks. "Gosh, I thought it'd take way more wooing before you'd want to kiss me, beautiful." He noticed me looking at his lips. Great. I must be as red as a tomato by now. I hate that I blush so visibly. Yet, he doesn't kiss me. I'm sort of relieved; I don't know if I can handle the guilt right now. Luc admitted he likes me, *we kissed.* It wouldn't be fair for me to kiss Alex right now.

"This place is beautiful. How have I never been here before?"

"Because it's a very big park, *with a stage, might I add.* This is my favourite area by far, though. Sitting under this little tree by the stream."

"I can just imagine sitting here for hours on end reading."

"I love that you find that fun. You and Caroline are so alike."

"What would your idea of fun be then? Right here, right now, what's fun?"

"My idea of fun would be jumping into that water, following it down to a larger river, and swimming."

"Do you enjoy being in the water?"

"More than anything. When I'm back in California, my favourite thing to do is surf. It makes me feel like me."

"You go there often?"

"Yeah, my Dad lives there. And I spend all summer there."

"Where in California?"

"He lives in LA. Right by the beach. So I've had plenty of time to practice surfing growing up. The waves are like family to me.

"That sounds lovely. You should take me someday; teach me to surf!" I say, smiling.

He grins. "That would be awesome, Ambre. I'd be honoured to teach you how to surf."

I pull my camera out of my bag. "Take a picture with me?" I'm making a scrapbook full of memories, so I aim to take as many pictures as possible.

Instead of answering, Alex pulls me to lie against his chest and takes the camera from my hands.

"Say cheese!"

I grin and pull a funny face. Alex winks.

"That's definitely a keeper. Can I keep this?"

"Why do you want to keep it?" I ask because I'm not sure what use he could find in a photo of us.

"I want to put it in my phone case." I think my heart just melted.

"I mean, I was going to scrapbook it, but yes. I suppose you can have it." I say, smiling to myself.

As I'm *discreetly* staring at Alex, well, I'm hoping it's discreet...

Music starts playing.

"There's a band here?"

"There's a reason I brought you here, beautiful."

'One of us' aka my favourite song of all time, starts playing. Now, if there's one way into my heart, it's Abba. Sing Abba songs with me, dance to them, and bring me to freaking see them live! And I'll love you forever.

"Alex, I freaking adore you. You're an angel." I say, gently hitting his arm, and as if on cue, *'Angel eyes'* starts playing.

Alex smiles and pulls me to hug him.

We spend the rest of our time dancing and singing along to the Abba songs. Alex dances with me! He dances with me. Twirls and everything. *He even has rhythm!*

I enjoyed today. I haven't thought about Luc once... until right now, that is.

Chapter 11

Ambre

Lucie has been staying at mine and Luc's apartment for the past week. I can't help but wonder if she's sleeping in my room or maybe with Luc? I don't know what would be worse.

I shouldn't say that. It wouldn't be all that bad if Luc and Lucie were to date, would it? It would mean he's moving on from his crush on me, which means things can go back to normal.

It just feels weird. The thought that the boy I've spent my entire life with is now basically living with some other girl. Just them. Living together. It's not permanent; obviously, that's my home. But it's been three weeks since the argument. Three weeks I've been here.

Do I call Luc? Do I go and get all my stuff? *Do I permanently move out?* Can I vote for none?

I'm sure he's feeling the same about me living here with Alex. I have no doubt that Lucie told him what she saw. Me and Alex in bed together. Yes, it looks bad. However, if she'd been there earlier, she would have seen we were just watching a movie. Nothing suspicious going on there.

On the subject of Alex, we have quite bonded. He's been telling me about his life back in California. His surfer boy days. He still surfs all the time. It sounds *epic*. As he says.

And as much as I'd love to forget everything around me and just consume myself in Alex's surfing stories, I can't ignore my reality. My best friend, whom I live with, is living with another girl in our home. I'm staying with Caroline and Alex. I haven't spoken with Luc in three weeks. I think that's the longest we've ever gone without speaking in our entire lives. That's scary.

It does still sting. Because as much as he's driven me bonkers, I miss him. I miss my loving, my sweet, fun best friend. It hurts to know that Lucie is getting that Luc, and I'm not.

He's the only guy that's ever been in my life. I'm the only girl that's ever been in his life. Now he's got Lucie. Now I've got Alex.

I wish I could say that this feels right. That I'm happy with things where they are. But that would be a lie.

I love love love living with Caroline. I adore getting to know Alex; I'm so glad that I'm getting to know these new people. Becoming *good* friends with them. But I'm also not naive. Luc is always going to be a part of my life, no matter what. Whether I want him in it or not. Because he's with Lucie now, dating or not. And Lucie is a part of this friend group, the one I'm now also a part of. Meaning that no matter what, I'll be seeing Luc. I'm confused. I miss him, but at the same time, I want nothing more than to never see his face again.

"Hey, girl, what you doing in here when the weather is like that? We rarely get sun; take advantage of it!"

"I will, I will. I'm just finishing this literature paper. Have you done it? The one where you've got to write five chapters of your book set in the 1700s?"

"Yes! Of course, I've done it. I was right on that the second it got assigned. I adore those assignments."

"And it has nothing to do with that fact you wanted to finish and hand it in before a certain rugby player?"

"Oh my Gosh. Don't even remind me of Beau. He is the devil's spawn, I swear. And it had nothing to with him! I finished before him, just in case you were wondering."

I laugh. "Of course you did. He was thrilled about that, I'm sure."

"Oh, he was ballistic. I saw him walking into the building as I was walking out. He glared, I smirked. It was great." She says this as if it were the greatest thing that's ever happened to her.

"I do love you, Care."

"Aw, I love you too boo! Speaking of *love*, nothing happened with you and lover boy?"

"I'm guessing lover boy is Luc?"

"Correct."

"Nothing's happened. We haven't spoken in three weeks. Not to mention he and Lucie have something going on now."

"I'm sorry, WHAT? Lucie told me she was staying over at her sister Elena's!"

"Oh. Why wouldn't she want you to know?"

"I don't know! But she wanted *you* to know. How did you find out?"

"She came back here wearing one of Luc's hoodies, got a bag of stuff and left. I've not seen her since."

"Oh no, she did not! How dare she! Steal your man's hoodie?! I love that girl to bits, but this is war. She used to have a thing for Alex. Make her jealous with him."

"Care. Honestly, it's fine. I'm the one who told Luc we can't happen. I stopped it. We kissed, and the next morning I told him I couldn't be with him."

"You what? Are you stupid!?"

"No, Care, I'm not," I say, a little sharper this time. "He is my-he *was* my best friend. I wasn't going to risk losing that for a relationship."

"Well, now you've gone and lost both. You know, if you were in a relationship, you would've had your best friend and life-long love. Girl, what have you done?"

"I was scared. And confused. I love him as my best friend so much. I'm scared to lose him and be alone."

"You already have lost him; if you don't go get him! you better go get that boy back! Salvage that friendship before it's too late. He's not coming for you, trust me. He put himself out there; he risked getting his heart broke. Do you understand how much courage that must have taken? You shot him down, Ambs. He's hurting. And Lucie is there consoling him, healing that broken heart when it should be you."

"You're right. I hate that you're right."

"Hunny, you'll soon realise I am always right." I laugh. She's not wrong there.

I may not be able to love Luc the way he wants me to, but I love him with everything I have. He's my person. He always has been. I'm going to go get my best friend back before it's too late.

Chapter 12

Ambre

So, as I expected, I have absolutely no idea what to say or what to do. Do I just show up at the apartment? How would that go down? Oh, hey, Luc! Yeah, let's be friends now after I rejected you multiple times and messed with your feelings! I don't think so.

I'm going to do the one thing I know I'm good at. I'll write Luc a letter.

Writing is my hobby; it's my future career, it's what I'm getting a degree in right now. Yet I can't seem to form the words. I don't think I even *know* how I really feel right now. But what I do know is that Luc is my best friend, and I will do anything to not lose him.

Okay,

Luc, I'm writing this because, as you know, I'm not too great with talking, and things are awkward enough as it is...

"Girl, what the hell are you doing?" Caroline's voice echoes from behind me. Scaring the living daylights out of me, might I add.

"I'm writing Luc a letter?"

Sarcastically she replies, "No, You don't say!"

I roll my eyes.

"I know you're writing a letter! What the hell are you writing, though!? Don't bring up past awkwardness. The point of this is to get rid of it. Put that in the bin, start again. Also, I'm not quite sure why you're handwriting it. I mean, it looks cute. Make sure he keeps it! Omg, can I scrapbook it once he's read it?" Caroline rambles on. I swear this girl could talk for flipping hours without breathing.

"Okay, okay slow down. One, fine! I will restart. You're helping, though! And two, no. No, you can not scrapbook this personal letter, Care."

"Ugh, fine. Right, let's start again. Start saying why you're writing to him. Without mentioning the past."

Luc, I'm writing this to you because I miss you. I miss you so much, and I messed up. By the time you're reading this, we may have already spoken, but in case we haven't, please keep reading.

"How's that?"

"Good! Keep going, don't make it awkward, and do what you do best, Ambs."

"What, write?"

"Write from your heart, babe." She blows a kiss.

"Okay, thank you, Care," I say, smiling. I can't express how much I love that girl.

You, Luc Bonet, are my best friend. I've never missed you more than I do right now. The thought of losing you has always scared me, terrified me even. Now, I'm scared I've already lost you. I never once imagined we'd ever be in such a situation, but hey, life has always loved to mess with us. We've been through so much together, we've got through it together, and this is just one more obstacle for us to overcome. I truly believe that we can overcome it. Because we are Ambre and Luc.

I feel like we should address the whole situation, but I'd rather talk to you in person. When we're living together once again. Which we will soon enough if you choose to forgive me.

It's me and you, Luc. It always will be. Please don't let this be the end of us.

I hope this is enough. I don't want to lose him.

I'm standing at the front door of my apartment, my real home, and I've never been more scared to knock on a door. What will I say if he answers?

I'm seriously debating just dropping this letter through the letter box. But I need to at least *try* to speak to him.

After giving myself a mini pep talk, I'm finally going to knock. I'm going to do it, I don't want to do it, but I'm going to do it. As I bring myself to knock, the door opens...

"Ambre, what are *you* doing here?"

Lucie answers. No Luc. It's Lucie. Why is Lucie answering the door to me? Where's Luc?

"Ambre, please explain why you've been pacing back and forth outside our apartment." Did she just say *our* apartment?

"I need to see Luc."

"Hun, Luc doesn't want to see you. And I don't exactly blame him." She says, looking me up and down.

"Yes, okay, I get that. But I *need* to see Luc. Please."

"Ambre, what don't you understand about *he doesn't want to see you*. Honestly, I don't think he ever wants to see your face again. Plus, he's not here right now. Even if he was, he wouldn't be talking to you."

"You know what, just give him these for me." I say, shoving the letter and flowers in her hand.

Luc and I made a pact back when we were thirteen.

Whenever I was upset, he'd buy me my favourite flowers. When Luc didn't know how to use words to comfort me, he got yellow and purple tulips. (Yellow symbolises brightness and happiness). To show me that no matter how down I'm feeling, the sun will come out again. (Purple, because it's my comfort colour). A colour that I'll never get tired of. It reminds me of music and books. And it's also a way of feeling closer to my nana: purple was her colour. Finally, tulips because they symbolise unconditional love and new beginnings. Luc, he doesn't give himself enough credit. He started doing this when we were only thirteen. And he's been doing it since. Whenever I'm mad, upset, or stressed, he gets flowers. To remind me everything is okay, even when he doesn't know how to tell me himself.

So I got Luc daisies. His Mam was called Daisy. I know Luc, he won't remember to water them every day, and then they'll die. Luc doesn't need to be reminded of any type of death. Especially by some Daisies. So I got him forever flowers. That's what I call them. They're just fabric and plastic flowers, but I think 'forever flowers' sounds prettier.

These daisies symbolise Daisy, Luc's Mam. daisies also symbolise purity and love. These being forever flowers show that I'll love him forever; my love will never die. And neither will his Mam's love.

As much as it hurts, I walk back to my temporary home without having spoken to my Luc.

A

I don't know what I was expecting to happen, but it wasn't that. I can feel my heart breaking. Is that it? Is this the end of Ambre and Luc for good?

I rush to my room, and the second my door closes, I stop holding it in. All the exhaustion of containing this. I let the tears fall, and they don't stop. All the stress building up to seeing Luc, and it went exactly how I prayed it wouldn't.

If only I knew what my heart was telling me. I could tell Luc how I feel. But I don't.

My arms wrap around my body, hugging myself, and my hands tremble as the tears continue to run down my face.

Someone knocks at my door. I wipe my eyes continuously, hoping they won't appear so red.

"Hey, pretty girl, it's me. Can I come in?" Alex.

"I'd rather be alone."

"Well, that's more of a reason for me to join you." He pushes the door open slowly.

He takes one look at my face, and he knows. I see his expression drop the second he sees my face.

"What the hell happened, Ambre? Are you okay?" He pulls me in for a hug.

"I- I think I've lost Luc."

"Ambre, I think any boy would be delusional to ever let you go, friendship or romantic."

"Alex, you don't understand."

"So help me understand. And let me comfort you for a while."

We sit on my bed. Alex pulls me into his chest, his hand resting on my head, pulling me close. All I can think of is how safe Luc's hugs make me feel. And how Alex hugs so differently to Luc.

Is it possible to miss a person's scent? I miss the way Luc smells, I miss his hugs that make me feel like nothing in this world could possibly hurt me, I miss running through the streets of Paris whilst the rain pours, with my Luc, I miss my home.

I sob, hard, into Alex's chest. My heart hurts. I can't even express how much this hurts. The feeling that you're losing someone forever, that somebody else is in the picture while you're not, I've never felt anything quite like it.

"Alex, I can't do it." My voice breaks.

"What can't you do, beautiful?" He stares down at me with soft, gentle eyes.

"Whatever little flirting thing we have, the date we went on, all of it, I can't."

"Ambs, I know." He says knowingly.

"What do you mean, you know?" I'm confused. He couldn't possibly know anything.

"I've always known. I just thought it was worth a shot."

"Known what?" I ask with slightly less patience this time.

"Your heart belongs to him. It always has." My heart belongs to Luc?

"Luc's my best friend."

"Ambre, I think we both know he's a lot more than just your best friend."

"He's not. He's always been my *best friend*; I just miss him so much. I've never gone this long without seeing him, or talking to him." A tear drops down my cheek and onto Alex's sleeve.

"You might not want to admit it to yourself, but it's so clear, Ambs. The way your eyes light up when he walks into a room. The way you hug him like it's your last each time. The way you look at him, It's *love*. Ambre, you're in deep."

"*Love* is a very strong word, Alex. Yes, of course, I love Luc. But I'm not *in love*. There's a difference between loving someone and being *in* love with someone."

"You're right; it is a powerful word. One that should be used so much more often. Tell people you love them, tell them after a week, hell, tell them after a day if you want. Never hold that word in when you feel it. It doesn't matter what type of love; if it's *love*, you tell them. I'd rather overuse 'love' than never use it at all."

"Wow, you can tell you've been living with Caroline." I say with a small smile.

"Oh, shut up." He smiles and rolls his eyes, " Maybe you're just not ready yet; that's okay. But you will be one day, trust me."

"Thank you, Alex. For being here and for understanding."

"Anytime, gorgeous. I'll gladly take the role of third best friend." He says with a wink as he leaves the room.

"Hey, Care?" I call from my room.

"Yes, my beloved Ambre?" She says, sticking her head into my room.

"You're allowed pets here, right?"

She looks at me questioningly. "Yes, why? What have you done?"

"Oh, I've not done anything yet."

"Okay then, let's rephrase. Ambre, what the hell are you planning?"

"I'm getting a cat." I say casually.

I figured a cat would make me feel better. I miss my cat. Bubba is back at home (I named him when I was six), and Ami is keeping him company. I couldn't bring him. It would be cruel, London is his home, and Ami is his person just as much as I am. So I figured I'll get Bubba a brother. A french kitty.

"Right. You're getting a cat? Just randomly decided you're getting a cat?"

"Exactly, yes."

"Let's go get a cat then, Hunny."

I squeal and clap my hands.

We arrive at the pet store, and I spot the cats through a door. I can't hold back my excitement.

Care talks for me, "Hey, can we go on through to the cats, please? My friend here is looking to adopt."

"Oui, continuer." She talks french back to Care. She must recognise her.

"Merci." We say together.

The faint sound of 'what makes you beautiful' plays quietly as we walk in. Care and I look at each other with wide eyes. Then as any sane person would, we perform a silent concert together, lipsyncing to the words and holding our invisible microphones. As the song finished, we laugh and head over to the cats.

"Omg, Ambs, this one's called Chubby. He's so freaking fat it's adorable. I love fat animals."

"Care, don't disrespect Chubby," I say, laughing. I walk over there and see that Chubby the cat is, in fact, very chubby. And he's adorable.

"Care, omg, I need him."

"I freaking told you!"

"And he's ginger. Just like my bubba back at home." I say in awe.

"Get him, girly. He's all yours now."

"I'm sold. Chubby, you are coming home with me." I say to Chubbs as he purrs away.

Chapter 13

Luc

Lucie and I head down to the cafe at about one. The cafe Ambre and I used to meet at every day after classes. Lucie insisted we come here for lunch instead of just having a homemade salad again. It just so happens everyone else is also here. And now we're sitting with them.

"Luc, I swear I had no idea they were here. If I knew, I wouldn't have insisted we come. Trust me, I don't want to see her just as much as you right now." Lucie whispers into my ear. It's us on one side of the booth, Ambre, Caroline and Alex on the other side. God, I feel like I'm about to get interrogated.

"It's fine. You didn't know."

"Well, long time no see, Lucie!" Caroline says, full of energy, as usual.

"Yeah, I know, right." Lucie says shyly. She clearly doesn't want to be here just as much as me.

"How's it been, man?" Alex asks me. Why is Alex talking to me as if we're friends? This is what I wanted to avoid.

"It's been fine. Thanks." I answer dryly.

Lucie, Caroline, and Alex chat for a while until we eventually order our food. The same waiter that served Ambre and I last time we were here serves us. I swear I see Ambre stiffen from the corner of my eye. It could just be in my head. I also notice that she doesn't say a word or even look my way. From the second I got here, she's been silent. How lovely, rejects her best friend, gives mixed signals, ruins our entire friendship, and doesn't even have the decency to ask how I've been?

For this entire hour, Caroline has done nothing but throw daggering eyes. Glaring at me as if I killed her puppy dog.

"Caroline, can I have a word over there?" I say sharply. I don't like drama. I sure as hell don't want to talk to Caroline, but I won't have her give me daggers for no bloody reason. I'm not the one who's done anything wrong here.

She moves out of the booth and joins me outside.

"What do you want, Luc?" She says, exasperated.

"No, no. You don't get to be the one who's annoyed here. I'm annoyed. What the hell is going on over there? Why are you glaring at me like I've killed someone?"

"You know damn well why Bonet."

"No, *Lavigne*, I don't. So please do enlighten me."

"Ambre put herself out there. Do you know how much courage that took her? She just wants you back. You could have replied and said no; at least that way, she'd have some closure."

"What the hell are you going on about?"

"Stop acting dumb. You know what I'm on about, Luc. I'm not going to explain just for you to act clueless again. If it wasn't already clear, I don't like you. Almost as much as I don't like Beau, and that's bloody saying something. You hurt my Ambre, so yes, I'm going to glare at you, and I won't apologise for it. Okay?" She says sharply and walks back inside.

I run my hands over my face, now I'm bloody exasperated. What is she going on about? I've not heard anything from Ambre in weeks.

I quickly search through my top drawer, well, Lucie's draw. I wouldn't usually do this because I feel like it's an invasion of privacy. However, I could've sworn I left my textbooks in this drawer. And I desperately need them to study for my class. I didn't do so great this term. I'm hoping after Christmas break, I can up my game. And a few nights before Christmas, not many campus bookstores are open; I don't know why. I'll most likely get kicked out if I show up to class again without having read it. As I'm rummaging through the drawer, I find a piece of paper with my name on it. Did I leave that in here by mistake? Maybe Lucie wrote something? I shouldn't read it; that could be a bloody love confession or a diary page, I don't know. As I'm about to forget about it and continue looking for the book, I notice not only my name but also Ambres on the back.

Luc, from your Ambre...

Now I would remember if I'd already read this. I wouldn't ever forget a letter written by *my am-* I mean Ambre. What is this? Underneath it is a bouquet...of daisies, with a note.

My Luc, to symbolise the purity that is our friendship and our never-ending bond. These Daisies carry not only my love but also your Mamas.

My Mama. God, I've not heard the word Mama in a while. I stopped calling her Mama and started saying Mam when boys in my class started bullying me, for one, being an orphan. No Mother or Father. Two, coming to school with bruises every day. Eric, the abusive stepfather that nobody tried to stop. And three, using Mama and Papa. They were French and wanted me to grow up with a bit of that still with me. So I stuck with Mama and Papa, that's who they are to me, and that's who they'll always be in heart.

I open the letter. This was written...two weeks ago? So why the hell would Lucie have this? And why would she hide it from me? My heart drops at what I read.

You, Luc Bonet, are my best friend. I've never missed you more than I do right now. The thought of losing you has always scared me, terrified me even. Now, I'm scared I've already lost you. I never once imagined we'd ever be in such a situation, but hey, life has always loved to mess with us. We've been through so much together, we've got through it together, and this is just one more obstacle for us to overcome. I truly believe that we can overcome it. Because we are Ambre and Luc.

I feel like we should address the whole situation, but I'd rather talk to you in person. When we're living together once again. Which we will soon enough if you choose to forgive me.

It's me and you, Luc. It always will be. Please don't let this be the end of us.

I need to find Ambre.

Chapter 14 🗼

Luc

I stand at the door of what is Ambre's current home. I'm
terrified to knock. She thinks I ignored her. All because Lucie
hid it from me. What am I going to do with Lucie after all this?
I knock hesitantly. The door opens, and Alex answers.

"I need to see Ambre."

"About bloody time. Only two weeks late, Luc."

"I didn't see the letter until today. Lucie kept it hidden from
me."

Alex scoffs. "Honestly, that doesn't surprise me. Lucie is
possessive, and she wants you."

"Ambre?"

"Right, yes, Ambre isn't here."

"What do you mean she's not here? Where else could she be?
There are no more classes now until January."

"She got a flight to London last night." He says with an
apologetic look.

I sigh and run my hands across my face. I'm going to go crazy.

"Please tell me you're going after her."

"Of course I bloody am," I say as if it was already implied.

"Don't let her get away this time, Luc. Girls like her are hard to find. And fortunately for you, she wants you."

I nod and jog back to my car.

I rush to my room to get a suitcase packed when I get home. I checked flights, and there's one leaving in two hours. It'll take forty minutes to get to the airport.

"Where are you going in such a rush?" Lucie.

"London."

"What? You're leaving? Why?" She sounds almost panicked.

"I'm going after Ambre, Lucie."

Her face pales. "Why would you go after Ambre? After everything she did."

"I found the letter."

She goes completely silent.

"Luc-"

"Lucie, to be honest, I don't care about anything you have to say right now. I'm going after my best friend. I'll deal with you when I'm home back in January. But, for now, please pack all your things and go home."

"January? Luc, I can't wait that long. Please, don't leave."
With that, I walk out the door.

Chapter 15 🗼

Ambre

Being back in London feels like a breath of fresh air. Paris is my
home, but London will always have a special place in my heart.
I've missed London. I've missed Ami. Ami is going to be ecstatic
when she meets chubbs. Yes, I got him a cat passport so he could
come with me.

I walk through the door of my old home and hear Ami
chattering to Mum in the living room. I walk in, and Ami
screams.

"Ambre, OMG." She shouts.

"Hey, mini me!" I squeal.

Ami jumps into my arms, and I squeeze them against me tightly.

"I've missed you so freaking much!"

"My girl, you've grown." My Mum says all emotional.

"Hey, Mum. I've missed your hugs so much." I say, hugging her
tightly. The top of her head rests just below my chin when I'm in
these heels.

"Hey, where's Luc? I've missed my little boy." My Mum looks confused. I'm not surprised. Luc has spent every Christmas with us since we were kids. He might as well be her son.

"Luc and I sort of fell out."

"You're joking, right?" Ami questions.

"Nope, not joking, Ami. I'm sorry; I know you both miss him."

"That's okay, baby. Know you can talk about it with us if you are ever ready." I appreciate that she says when I'm ready. She never makes us feel pressured to talk.

"Yes, that. Of course that. But also I kind of-"

"Yes, Ami. I will give you the gossip. Promise."

She smiles. "Thanks."

"Right, my girls. Enough chit-chat about Luc. Let me hear about Paris! Gosh, I miss that city. Paris was my home for a very long time. It always will be home in my heart."

"Okay, I'm jealous now. I want to see Paris!" Ami exclaims.

"Okay, okay. Chill mini-me. When I go home, I suppose you could come with me. If Mum is okay with that, of course."

"O.M.G.", She squeals. "Mum, can I? Can I?"

"As long as you stay out of trouble, I don't see a problem with it. If Ambre is sure."

"I'm sure. You can bunk with me in my room."

"I'm all of a sudden dying for it to be January. Sorry, December!" Me and Mum both laugh. Ami is the light in every room.

"Ambs, can we go shopping for the Christmas party? I want an eye-catching dress. Mum's friend has an insanely cute son. He's like a year older but whatever."

"Www, spill. What's his name?" I have missed these little gossip sessions with Ami.

"He's called Rhys. And he is so hot."

"And that is my cue to leave. I'll be making tea."

We both laugh as she walks out of the room. "Tell me more."

We sit on the living room floor gossiping about everything, catching each other up on anything we've missed. I filled Ami in on the Luc situation. Safe to say, she was ecstatic when I told her we kissed...a few times. And she says we're endgame, despite everything that's happened. I also tell her about Caroline, Alex, and Lucie. Caroline, she claims Caroline as her new bestie. Alex, she asks if he's hot and single. And Lucie, she's not very fond of. Once tea is ready, we sit at the dining table watching Pride and Prejudice. And I feel genuinely okay. Which I haven't in a while. At this moment, I feel safe, back with my family, back in my home, back into our usual routine.

They also love Chubbs with every fibre of their beings (Ami words), And I got to give Bubba a long-needed cuddle. "Goodnight, my lovelies. Get plenty of rest, long day of shopping tomorrow!"

And everyone heads to bed. The wave of nostalgia hits me the second I go into my room. I've not been gone that long but seeing my old posters, my CDs, reading old diaries, I realise how much I've changed since being in Paris, and also how much I'm still me, if that makes sense. I'm still this girl who adores music, who would fan girl over a boy band until the day she dies, the girl who finds comfort in a book or in a song, the girl who would kill for a novel-worthy romance. However, I'm no longer the girl who's terrified of speaking to new people. I'm now accustomed to change, and it doesn't scare me. I've got the mindset of never holding back and being honest with myself. Well, I'm still working on that last one. But I'm getting there. I've missed everything so much. But I wouldn't for a second go back. Paris is my home now, and it always will be.

I snuggle up to Chubbs and Bubba in bed and read my book before going to sleep. Turns out they don't hate each other. Bubba has always been extremely welcoming.

"Ambre! Look how hot this dress is!" I walk to Ami and see what dress has caught her attention this time. We've been through about twenty already.

"Wow, yeah, it's super hot. I'll buy it for your eighteenth birthday." Her jaw drops.

"What! Why not now? Eighteen, seriously?"

"Ami, I think Mum would kill both of us if you showed up to the party wearing that dress. Especially considering it's to impress Rhys."

"Well, I see nothing wrong with this beautiful dress." She says, turning her nose up at me.

"Yeah, sure. The v-neck on that, not even I could fill that, Ami. And I'll be nineteen next month. Not to mention the considerably short length. Don't get me wrong, Ami, you'd look fire in that dress, just not in front of Mum."

"Okay, I won't wear it in front of her then. And if she ever finds out, I'll say you didn't have any idea I got it."

I roll my eyes and smile. Persistent is one way to describe Amélie de Roselle. "Deal."

She squeals in excitement. "I love you, Ambs. Best sister ever."

I flip my hair back dramatically. "I know, right." We smile at one another. Moments like these with my sister make me consider staying here in London. Spending the rest of my days here with my favourite person.

In the end, we did both find a dress. Dresses that are more appropriate for a family Christmas party. Before our Mum got a chance to see Ami's little red dress, I paid, and we left with our dresses packaged up.

The rest of the day gets spent buying decorations and snacks, which Ami and I eat most of on the way home.

"Girls, for heaven's sake, leave some snacks for the guests." She says, smiling into the rear-view mirror.

"I don't know what you're on about," Ami says as she shoves another crisp in her mouth. "This car ride is dead; I'm connecting my playlist."

My Mum shakes her head whilst smiling. "Here we go again."

"That, mother dearest, is an excellent suggestion." Ami says with a mockingly posh accent as 'Mamma Mia' comes on. Our family are definitely Abba fans. We spend the rest of the car ride screaming Mamma Mia with the windows down and flakes of snow falling outside.

"Oh, Ambre, I forgot to mention that we've rented a much fancier venue for the party this year." She says proudly. It melts my heart seeing her so prideful and happy. It's been a while.

"Why's that? I thought everyone was fine having it at our place."

"They are, of course. But I wanted to spice it up this year. And make it a special homecoming for you. We weren't expecting you so early either!"

"I wasn't planning to be home so early, to be honest. My plans got messed with a little. I wasn't sure if Luc was still planning on coming home for Christmas, and I sure as hell was not sitting on a plane with him for hours. So I came early." I say with a shrug. I'm trying to seem careless about the whole situation; I don't know if it's working.

"Oh, Hunny, things will work out. I promise you. Friendships like yours don't end over a silly argument."

I manage a faint smile, "Thanks, Mum." She returns a pitying smile.

Tonight feels different to last night. Last night, I was on a high. I felt good finally knowing who I am, who I've become since being away. Tonight, I feel lonely. I miss Luc so freaking much. This time of year, I'm usually sitting here talking to Luc about everything and nothing all at once. We'd sit here and play vinyl together until we couldn't possibly listen to Taylor Swift again.

Then, after all that's over, we'd go outside and have a snowball fight. No matter the time. It was dark and freezing cold, yet being outside with Luc on a snowy night, was the highlight of my day, of my month, and even of my year. I will always always treasure Winters with my Luc. If I can even call him mine anymore. He may not be mine romantically; however, he's always been mine. My best friend, my person, my world.

I need to take my mind away from real life. Real life is too much effort. Picking up my comfort read is always the solution. She's looking a little worn down now, full of tabs, annotations, and even a broken spine. However, I have a reason for this.

Trust me, I would never intentionally break a spine. But, when I was about thirteen, my Nana gave me her favourite book. She said that book was her home and her escape from everything. I'd never used to be a reader, but my Nana was my idol, so I read it for her. And sure enough, it sparked my love for reading.

It's not even my usual type of read, either. I read romance, contemporary romance, usually. This book is a new adult fantasy about pirates. My Nana didn't seem to mind me reading a book meant for an older reading group, so neither did I. This book captured me from the very first sentence. I read it in one sitting. Now, whenever I need an escape from reality, I return to this book. This book reminds me of my Nana and makes me feel close to her. Each time I read this, I fall in love with the characters all over again, and each time it's like we're living in this fantasy world together. No reality in sight. Just me, my Nana, and the pirates. It's my escapism.

After my re-read, I decide to sleep. Chubbs on my pillow, Bubba at my side, we fall asleep within seconds.

Chapter 16 🗼

Ambre

Day of the party. One of my favourite nights of the year, usually.
I dress up; I feel genuinely beautiful. Luc makes me feel
beautiful. We dance together all night, we eat way too much, and
we sing for hours on end. It's amazing. Except this year, I won't
have Luc to do all these things with.

"Ambs! Stop moping, you look hot AF in that dress, and your
droopy look is killing the vibe." Ami states whilst rolling her
eyes.

"I'm very sorry for my droopy look," I add sarcastically.

She looks at me sympathetically. God, I do not want sympathy
right now. Though I could use a hug.

"It's about Luc, isn't it? If you're worried about being alone
tonight, then I can get Rhys's older brother to dance with you.
He was my first choice, but Mum says three years is too much
for a fourteen-year-old." She rolls her eyes dramatically.

"I'm okay Ami, honest. I'll just sit out and get cute pictures of
you and Rhys."

She grins, "Aw, you're the best sister ever. Make sure I look good, okay."

"Of course." I add as if it wasn't already obvious.

Ami comes over to me and wraps her arms around my waist. I hug her tightly. My mini-me.

"I love you, Ambs. I've missed you so much."

"I love you too, Ami, so so much" She smiles sweetly at me. She may be sassy, but she's the sweetest girl I know.

Later in the evening, I put my dress on, hoping it still fits all snug after eating too much today. It does. It's a long pastel blue dress. It nearly touches the floor. The top has a little lace and a small v-neck. It's beautiful, and it's very me. I feel like a princess in this dress.

Ami comes in and does light makeup on me. Some faint baby blue eyeshadow following my eyeliner and mascara, and some highlights. Simple, yet effective. And I wear my blue bracelet Luc gave me when we were eight. Because 'it's an Ambre colour,' he says.

I can't possibly tame my curls even if I try, so I let them be crazy and free. And I almost agree with my sister's recent statement; I do look kind of hot. I haven't felt even an ounce of confidence in so long. This is pretty huge.

I walk downstairs, and Mum is rushing about trying to get everything into the car; we set everything up earlier. However, she insists we bring more food. So I grab a bag, and off we go. Ami wears a flowy pastel pink dress. It stops mid-thigh, so not as revealing as her first choice. And the top has beautiful sleeves with lace snowflakes on them. She looks gorgeous and so grown up it makes me want to cry. And my Mum wears a dark satin green dress, she is already crying.

"My girls, you look beautiful. So perfect. Gosh, please stop growing up on me so fast."

Ami and I share a smile.

Christmas music blasts over the entire 'party hall' as my Mum calls it. Everyone sings along to them, all of us ecstatic for Christmas tomorrow. Our extensive group of friends has always been merry during the holidays. And I love that it keeps the magic of Christmas alive. And let's be honest, Christmas music is the best part of Christmas altogether.

More and more people come to the de Roselles' annual Christmas party each year now. It was just a few close friends and family, then Ami started inviting her friends, people on the street heard about it, and soon enough, we had a very packed house. The party hall was a good idea.

I want to love tonight. I love tonight, just not as much as I would if Luc had been with me. I need to move on from Luc. He ignored me. I have to live with the fact that this might well be the end.

The end of Luc and Ambre.

My heart cracks just at the thought. I tried to get him back. I went to our- his house, I got him flowers, a wrote a freaking letter, I honestly don't know what much more I could do. All I know is that I need him back.

"Merry Christmas eve, everyone! Before we do *the dance* of the evening, the dance that all couples and friends look forward to all year, let's all make a Christmas wish. Everyone throws a penny into the fountain and makes a wish. Then the dance will start!" My Mums cheery voice echoes through the speakers; yes she got freaking speakers for this thing. I love her.

Everyone begins to flick pennies into the fountain, I take mine out, and I put every last piece of hope I have inside me into this wish.

I need my Luc back.

Merry Christmas eve, Luc. Whatever you may be doing.

Alps by Nova Amor plays loudly through the speakers.

Every couple or friendship duo get together for this dance. We all know this is a love song. However, some of us choose to give that love to our friends instead. As Luc and I do every year, except this one.

I stand in the corner of the room, drinking a glass of bucks fizz: Christmas tradition. Watching everyone else look at each other so full of love and admiration, it hurts that I'm not with them doing that. As promised, I got the perfect picture of Ami and Rhys slow dancing.

A tear escapes and runs down my cheek. I dab it away quickly before ruining someone else's mood. I hate that I feel this way. I hate that I miss him so much.

I freeze as I feel a light tap on my shoulder.

"Can I have this dance?" A deep, shaky voice asks me.

"Luc." I stare at him in disbelief. He's here, in London, standing right in front of me. "You're here."

A sombre look fills his eyes. "Princess, of course, I'm here."

And just like that, crack: healed.

"You're calling me princess again?" I ask, my voice filled with way too much hope.

"I'll always call you Princess. You are my princess."

"God, I've missed you, Luc." I throw my arms around his neck, he pulls me in tightly. He is holding me like he's scared to let go. I'm afraid this is a dream, and if I let go, it'll all be over. I can't lose this again.

"Let's go dance; there's not long left before the song finishes." He grabs my hand and pulls me over to where everyone is dancing. And we join the flow, dancing, swaying, twirling, smiling because we're genuinely happy.

"I still can't believe you're here," I say to him as we walk over to a more hidden table.

"I wouldn't have missed it for the world." He rubs his thumb across the palm of my hand.

"You read my letter then?" I ask warily.

"I did. God, I'm sorry I didn't see it earlier. Of course, I would have spoken to you. I'd never ignore you, Ambre. Never." He states with an apologetic look on his face.

"Why didn't you see it, though?"

"Lucie." He says as if she's a sore subject.

"Oh." I look down; I don't need him seeing any envious look on my face at her mention.

"I told her to pack up her things and leave."

This brings my head back up and sparks some hope inside of me. I can't quite place what this hope is, but it's hope. "So she's gone?"

"Well, I'm assuming she'll return to stay with Caroline and Alexandre, and you'll come home." He suggests with hope in his voice. "Unless, of course, you want to stay with Caroline."

"Luc, I'm coming home." I smile. He looks at me with a grateful expression. "Oh, and so is Ami! I told her she could come back with me."

He nods vigorously, "That sounds perfect, Ambre." Then, looking into my eyes, he smiles. I didn't realise how much I missed these smiles being for me.

I decide to approach the subject we both desperately want to avoid. "So, I know this isn't really what either of us wants to talk about right now, but we probably should talk about *us*."

"No, I agree. Later tonight? I want to enjoy this party with you. Just like old times."

"Let's do it." I say and pull him over to the drinks. Apparently, I eat when stressed, and I drink when nervous.

I sit on my bed with my legs crossed, and Luc sits in my egg chair in the corner; we both stare down awkwardly. This night has been amazing. However, now we're back to reality. A place neither of us really wants to be.

"I'm sorry, Luc." It comes out rushed and shaky. I rub my clammy hands on my dress and fidget with the corner of my blanket.

"Ambs, please don't apologise."

"No, Luc, I hurt you. Because I couldn't understand my own feelings."

"Do you understand them now?" He asks while continuing to stare down.

"Not really. I've been thinking so much, trying to make sense of everything, yet I'm just as confused as ever." Luc and I don't once make eye contact. I underestimated just how awkward and painful this conversation would be.

"Okay, think out loud with me. Tell me everything, and maybe I can help you make sense of some of it."

My heart beats uncontrollably in my chest at what I'm about to say; I have to be honest. "I find you extremely attractive for one." My words come out rushed, and surely pink fills my cheeks. This doesn't go unnoticed by Luc.

Luc smirks at me, "Sorry, can you repeat that? I didn't quite hear you."

I roll my eyes and smile down to myself, "I find you hot." I say slower this time.

"That's not exactly hard, princess." He sits up and uncrosses his arms. Someone is finding his confidence.

"I find you attractive, I enjoy kissing you, and I adore our friendship so much. That's about as much as I know."

"So, we have chemistry, is what I'm getting." He adds thoughtfully.

"I guess so, yes." I look up for the first time. Luc stares at me heatedly until I catch him, and he turns away instantly. Surely I'm imagining that look, right?

"I know I love you," He sees the look of panic cross my face before adding, "As a friend, stupid. And I'd hope you bloody love me too."

I smile at him, "Of course, I love you, Luc."

"Maybe I was in over my head when I suggested a relationship. I love you as my Ambre, that's all, though. We have chemistry, but you were right. Some amazing kisses aren't worth risking our friendship over. And I'm sorry for overreacting when you were being smart. I've missed my best friend like hell."

A pang of hurt enters my chest when Luc says he, in fact, does not have feelings for me. Surely I should be happy. I was right, we're friends, and we shouldn't risk losing a friendship over chemistry. I guess living with a hot, interesting, new girl will help someone move on swiftly. I'm not fond of this feeling. Whatever it is, I want it gone. Things can finally go back to normal now. I *won't ruin that. I can't.*

Luc must notice the look on my face; he looks at me, confused.

"Exactly. We may have some crazy sexual tension, but we are friends!" Why, why, why did I say that? God, tone it down a bit, Ambre.

"Sexual tension? Isn't that like all you go on about when talking about books?" He asks smugly.

"Yes. Shut up."

"Hm, friends to lovers, right?" He smirks smugly. And looks way too proud of himself.

"Luc, shut up, or I'll do it for you." Okay, that sounded weird, didn't it? Is it me? Am I assuming everything is weird now? Well, everything *is* weird now.

"Okay, okay. My sincere apologies." He puts his hands up in a surrender movement. I shake my head smiling down at myself. I didn't know it was possible to miss one person so much.

"Luc, will we ever be normal again?" My voice breaks as I desperately try to hide the emotion in my voice.

"Princess, we are normal. Nothing has to change. It's all okay." He opens his arms and gestures me over.

I let myself fall into his arms and hold on tight.

"It's not been the same without you. Nobody's been there to talk my head off about books." I gently hit his shoulder.

Dramatically I answer, "See, you should never complain about my love for books, or you may never get another rant again, and how devastating would that be?"

Luc looks down at me with a genuine look of love in his eyes. My best friend. "So so devastating, princess."

"You know, I think 'princess' is growing on me."

"Oh, Ambre. 'Princess' has never needed to grow on you. You've always loved it." He winks down at me.

I shake my head, looking down.

"Can you stay here, please?"

"Well, unless you plan to kick me out into the shed, of bloody course, I'm staying here."

"Obviously! I mean here. Like, right here. Just let me cuddle you all night."

"Anything."

Right answer. Because my eyes are heavy with sleep and I don't think I could move if I tried. I won't admit it to Luc, but I'll sleep so much better if I'm close to Luc. He makes me feel safe. Like nothing, and *nobody* can hurt me. He's my person, and he always will be. My worries about losing my Luc drift away; I've never been so grateful.

Luc

If I could go back to any night, it would be the night Ambre, and I became best friends. I don't remember it clearly, considering we were kids, but I remember feeling whole for the first time in my life. Every second I've spent with Ambre has been phenomenal. I'll cherish every moment for the rest of my life. Even the ones where we've fought. Because we overcame it each time. Because we're Ambre and Luc.

As much as I think Ambre and I would make a damn fantastic couple, she doesn't want that. So I have to respect that, and I won't push again. One thing I can't comprehend is the way she looks at me. With so much freaking love, yes, I get that; we're best friends. But the way she looks at me, no matter how hard she tries to deny it, to herself and me, friends *don't* look at friends that way.

Yet, I'm terrified if I ever said anything like that again, I may just lose her all over again. I can't go through that again. I'm holding on because I need her. I don't want to let go of our friendship. And I'm not strong enough to survive losing her again, losing her forever.

I want her, I need her, and I long for her. My best friend, my forever,

my right person, wrong time.

"Luc, I love you so much." A sleepy voice brings my attention back to my reality, a sleepy Ambre laying cuddled up to me, on my lap. *My friend.*

"I love you so much too, princess. So god damn much."

Fortunately for me, she's half asleep and doesn't notice how my voice shakes. And how a silent tear escapes the corner of my eye.

Chapter 17 🗼

Ambre

My eyes open as I feel like I'm in an earthquake in my bed.
"Whoever is shaking me awake before ten am, kindly stop and let
me freaking sleep." I attempt to say, but the words come out
sleepily.

"Good morning to you as well, sunshine." A rather perky voice
replies. Light blinds me as I attempt to open my heavy eyes. To
my surprise, I find green eyes and a huge grin smiling down at
me, not Luc.

I rush to sit up, and a huge smile breaks free. I'm not so tired
anymore. "*Caroline?* What the hell are you doing in London?"
Wrapping my arms around her neck, I squeeze her and pull her
to lie next to me.

"I'm here to spend Christmas with my best friend, freaking
duh!" She smacks a big kiss on my cheek, leaving her lip gloss all
over my cheek. "Oops," a soft cotton sleeve wipes at my cheek;
yep, I'm covered in lip gloss.

A small laugh leaves my mouth, along with a happy groan.

"God, I've missed you! How are you here? I thought you had plans and couldn't make it."

"Well, *somebody* got me a last-minute plane ticket to surprise you." Care nods her head towards the tall masculine frame filling the doorway.

I slowly stand up, careful not to fall backwards, as I am still very full of sleep. "You did this? You brought my best friend here?" I ask, approaching Luc. I wrap my arms around his neck and whisper in his ear, "Thank you, Luc. I love you so much." He looks down at me with eyes full of love and sincerity before releasing me.

"Well, no. I brought your *second* best friend here." He winks at me with a half smile on his face. Caroline and I both laugh.

"I suppose I don't hate you anymore, Bonet. Don't get me wrong, you're definitely going to need to butter me up some more before I fully forgive you, but you made my Ambre happy. And that's what matters." I smack a big kiss on Caroline's cheek, returning the favour. Unfortunately, mine doesn't leave a lipstick or gloss mark.

"Incoming." Luc nods towards Amélie's bedroom in warning. Of course, a few seconds later a bundle of energy comes rushing into the room and throws herself on the bed.

"Goood morning, everyone!! Isn't the weather just amazing?" She sighs dramatically.

"Babe, it's raining and snowing... of freaking course it's amazing!!" Caroline answers with just as much enthusiasm. These two are going to get along. Luc and I laugh and shake our heads together.

"Oh my, God." Everyone stares at me expectedly. "Merry Christmas, everyone!"

"Merry Christmas!" Everyone shouts together.

"It's official, I'm coming to your house for Christmas every year from now on. That breakfast your Mum made, to freaking die for!" Caroline states whilst creating a ball of snow.

"Care, that would be the best Christmas gift ever. Please do."

"What, better than the infinity necklace?" Care eyes me suspiciously.

"Www, that's a hard one. I'm not sure if anything could top that," I say, my voice full of sarcasm. "And-"

Before I could continue, an icy ball hits the back of my bare neck. Unfortunately, I made the mistake of wearing my hair in a bun, exposing my neck to the chilly London snow.

Laughing, I aim my snowball at Care's head. "You little bi-"

"Ah, ah ah! No swearing in front of Ami." She runs and ducks behind a bench, shielding herself from my snowball.

"I was not going to swear!"

"You so were Ambs." Ami cuts in.

"Hush, you're on my side," I say jokingly while pulling Ami to my side. We whisper and plan how to win this battle. Ami forces Luc over to team with Care, hopefully bringing them closer, so it's less awkward.

Ami and I continue strategising, and then another snowball hits my head. And my back, and my legs. Yep, they're winning. I refuse to lose; we will win this. I rush Ami behind a phone box. Our hiding spot is way better than theirs; surely we can win now. Snow falls heavily, coating our hats and jackets with flakes of snow. And before we could declare a winner, it begins to rain heavily, drenching us through our jackets. It's a good job the de Roselles' have always loved the rain.

"Truce! It's bloody chucking it down!" Luc calls over from their hiding spot.

"Nuh-uh. I don't think so. We are not stopping because of some rain. You scared little Luc?" I mock him by putting my bottom lip out; provoking him will guarantee the game goes on. Luc doesn't like backing down or losing.

A smirk pulls down at his lips. "Ambre, love. We both know there's nothing little about me." He winks. He says this to throw me off, and God damn it, it works. I feel a blush rush to my cheeks. Luckily, I have the cold to blame for that.

Cockily, Luc returns to Caroline, thinking he won that conversation. As he's surely about to tell Care how he got into my head, throwing us off our game, I hit him with the biggest snowball I can manage to throw. And... bullseye! Right on the back of his head, knocking off his loose hat.

"You're going to pay for that, de Roselle." Luc heads towards me in big strides. But, before I can duck down, he reaches me and throws me over his shoulder. How the hell?

"This is cheating! You can't touch the other team! Or pick them up; that shouldn't even need to be said, come on." I whine. Purely because there is nothing else I can do right now other than kick. And as funny as it would be, I don't want to kick Luc's face; he hasn't annoyed me enough for that yet.

With no warning, I'm thrown into a big blanket of snow. Luckily, it's thick. So that felt like being thrown onto a fluffy blanket. However, I'm going to play this my way.

"Holy crap, ow. The floor, Luc! I think I need to go lie down; I feel dizzy." I exclaimed dramatically. I'll make this as drastic as I possibly can. As I go to stand up, Luc ushers me back down.

"I'm so sorry. Are you okay, princess? Sit down, let me check your head, don't move." I struggle to fight a grin, and Care notices. As Luc panics and searches my face for any sign of pain or confusion, Caroline bursts out laughing. "Caroline, will you bloody shut up! This isn't funny; Ambre might be hurt!" I fought to hide the grin, I failed.

"Luc, hunny. Ambre just played you. And you fell for it." Luc drags his hands down his face and rubs his forehead.

"You okay there, buddy?" I question him whilst trying to contain my laughter.

"You scared me." He says so quietly it might as well be a whisper. Quiet enough so only I can hear. "I thought you were hurt. If I ever did that to you, I couldn't live with myself."

I grab his face in my hands and look him in his eyes, "Luc, I'm all good. I promise. I'm sorry for scaring you."

"Jesus, Ambre. Don't do that again. Come here." With that, I'm pulled into a warm, hard chest.

"I'm bored of watching these two be in love with each other. Can we go ice skating or something?" Caroline lightly smacks the back of Amélie's head and shakes her head at her whilst laughing. "What? I swear everyone can see it except them; it drives me mad. I mean, they've always been close, but this is different. I can feel the chemistry! And I failed my last Chem exam!" Caroline bursts out laughing and wipes a tear from the corner of her eye.

"This kid, she is my best friend." Care says between laughs. While Ami smiles proudly.

As requested by Ami, we are going ice skating. Whilst Ami and Caroline are deep in conversation, Luc pulls me aside.

He's got a worried expression on his face, so naturally, I'm worried. "This is stupid, right? I say we go home and watch movies instead. Come on." He pulls at my arm, attempting to guide me to the door.

I giggle at him. What has gotten into this boy? "What's going on?" I ask suspiciously.

"I think ice skating is stupid, as I just said." Not once during this conversation has Luc looked into my eyes.

"No, Luc, what's wrong? Ice skating is not stupid. Why don't you want to be here?"

Luc's cheeks flush a light pink. Is he embarrassed? "I don't know how to skate." He whispers so quietly it's barely audible.

"Oh, Luc, that's fine! You can have a little penguin to skate with!" I joke, yet he doesn't realise this and looks mortified; it's hilarious messing with this boy.

"So, movie, yeah?" he begins walking towards the exit. I rush after him and drag him back by his arm.

"I'm joking. I'll hold your hand; we'll do it together, okay? That way, if one of us goes down, we go down together." He nods his head, clearly trying to convince himself more than me.

"Okay, yeah. I can do this."

"Of course, you can. Now, come on."

Luc

Being on the ice isn't as bad as I initially thought it might be. Knowing I have Ambre guiding me does make me feel a whole lot better, though. Once I've got the rhythm of it, ice skating is unexpectedly quite fun. We haven't even fallen yet, which is a bonus and a shocker. Caroline and Amélie are of skating around, looking like professionals, whilst poor Ambre is stuck monitoring me.

"I'm sorry you're not off skating like a pro with Ami and Caroline."

"Hey, don't worry about that. They may look pretty damn cool, but we look like an adorable couple, and I bet everyone is jealous of us right now."

From behind, I'm pushed forward without warning. Almost smashing my head against the ice as I'm thrown to the ground. Ambre flies forward with me and then lands on my back. My head is mere inches from hitting the ground and causing what would look like a crime scene.

What the hell just happened?

"Dad! Dad, stop! That's my brother!"

Henry? My brother? It can't be.

"Well, look what the cat dragged in. What are you doing back in London, Luc? I thought you were off to stay in Paris. Couldn't commit?" He stares at me, a malicious smirk pulling at his lips. "Doesn't surprise me, to be honest. Nobody in your family can commit to anything, not even *life* apparently." His venomous laugh echoes across the ice rink. He's drunk.

"Eric. I advise you to walk away right now, or-" Ambre's calm voice warns him before she gets cut off.

"Or what, barbie doll? You going to hurt me? We both know I could break your skinny little arms off right now with this blade if I wanted to, so watch yourself." *Did he just threaten my Ambre?* I wasn't going to make a scene for Henry and Amélie's sake. But now? Now he's got it coming.

Ambre gets herself up and drags me up with her. Before Eric can do or say anything else, Ambre quickly guides me off the rink with her.

"Are you okay, princess? Did you get hurt?" My eyes frantically search for injuries on her.

"Just a few scratches. I'll be okay. Are you okay? You took most of my fall." How can she be worried about me when that vile man just threatened her like that?

"Luc! I'm so sorry; I didn't know my Dad would do that." His voice breaks mid-sentence, "He's not like that usually. I don't understand. I just wanted to come over and say hi, then he did *that*." My baby brother.

The confusion and hurt in his voice breaks my heart. Eric and I may despise one another, but to show it in front of Henry, that's a new low, even for Eric.

"I've missed you, buddy," I say, raking my hand through his hair. "Don't you ever apologise for Eric's actions, you hear me?"

"Henry, get over here. What crap is this idiot trying to fill your head with? I need another beer for this. Damn it, Luc! This is your fault. You had to show your face. Where's the bar?" He slurs as he makes his way over to us. I pull Henry closer to my side. There's no way in hell I'm letting Henry go back to him. Of course, he's still a raging alcoholic. I never expected that to change. What I did expect was for him to be responsible enough to not drink when he's spending the day with my baby brother and *driving* him around.

Henry is not going home with him, not today, not ever. I'm not leaving Henry with him again.

As much as I try to keep myself calm for Henry's sake, it doesn't work. You know what? Screw being calm and mature. Sometimes the devil on your shoulder is right. And this? Oh, this definitely is one of those times.

I turn around and face Eric. Before he can say anything, I throw my fist into his face as hard as possible, leaving a nasty gush on his cheek. Blood drips down his face and onto the floor. Ouch, I forgot I had a ring on. Shame.

"That one's for my Mama because she's not here to do it herself,"

I grab his fist as he comes to strike me and bend his arm backwards until it'll need serious care. "That's for making my life a living hell," That felt amazing.

And there's one more thing. Depending on how it goes, I could be arrested. But I'm done playing it safe.

Without hesitation, I grab a skate from the floor and strike Eric in the forehead with it. The sharp edge should've been used, but I didn't, even though he deserves it. Sounds of shock and fear erupt around the rink. "And that one, that one's for hurting my Ambre. And making her life hell just as much as mine." With that, I leave him by flipping him off.

"You little sh-" He lifts his hand up to reach for me, and that's when he's grabbed.

I smirk at him as the officers come up behind him and handcuff him. "You're under arrest for fraud, and suspicion of child abuse. Anything you say or do can be held against you in a court of law." As the officers guide him out the door and he's forced into the police car, it finally hits me.

He's gone. He's actually gone. We're free.

Before doing anything else, I pull Henry to me, and I hug him hard. I know this is going to be hard on him. I just hope one day he knows it's for the better. He doesn't need that man in his life.

It's bloody hard not having a father figure there. *But it's also hard having a crappy one who is there.* "You're going to live with Ami and auntie for a while, okay, bud? You'll be safe and happy there, I promise." Ambre's Mum is mine and Henry's Godmother, so now that Eric's gone, he can live with her. He doesn't talk; he silently nods his head. I can see all the emotions running through his head right now. *I'm so sorry bud.*

Chapter 18 🗼

Ambre

"Luc, how did the police know to investigate Eric?" I whisper. This isn't the best time for questions but I'm so curious it hurts. "I had a couple of episodes, flashbacks to those days. Something triggered me, and they keep coming back. I can't survive them, to get rid of them I need him gone, out of my life, out of Henry's life. So I called the police a few weeks ago, I told them everything from the abuse, to the threats, everything. They said they had stuff on him anyway, and this will add to it greatly so they can take him in for questioning. I guess someone at the ice-rink saw him trying to cause a fight, so they called the police. Lucky for them, they had enough to arrest him and hopefully lock him up."

"I'm proud of you, Luc. So so proud." He smiles appreciatively at me.

We sit silently now in the police station, waiting for Luc, Henry and I to make a statement. They're going to need the whole truth from Luc and I. But there are some things about Eric I haven't told anyone, including Luc. I'm scared. Scratch scared, I'm petrified. What if Eric gets out? If he finds out, I told them he'll kill me. He will quite literally commit murder. *I need to tell Luc*; I know that. But if I tell Luc, *he'll* be the one committing murder.

"Madam de Roselle, Monsieur Bonet, please follow me." Luc puts his arm on my back and guides me out of the room. He knows I'm anxious. He just doesn't know the exact reason why. Before the officer could say anything else, I cut in, "So, are we doing this together or separate?" I blurt out as casually as possible, making it seem all the less casual.

"We will be doing this together today. We'd like to hear about your experience of Eric together. However, if there is any reason you'd feel uncomfortable talking in front of Luc, we will ask him to leave the room."

Luc eyes me suspiciously, does he know? He knows, doesn't he? "No, we're okay together. Thanks, though." He replies. Then whispers to me, "Ambs, what has got into you?"

Before I can reply, we get cut across. "Ambre de Roselle. We would like to start with you."

"Me? Are you sure? I'm sure Luc has a lot more information you need." I feel my face heating up and the blood rising to my head.

My hands begin the sweat as I rub them up my jeans in an attempt to dry them.

"That is exactly why we want Luc after you. We can get any information you might have. Then, once Luc is talking, if he deems something too personal or does not want you hearing about it, we can send you out and not have to bring you back in." I decide to drop it. If I carry on, Luc will be suspicious. Not that he'll need to in a minute. The secret will be out.

"Do you personally have any experience with the abuse of Eric? Physically, sexually, or verbally?" A tear drips down my cheek onto the table. Luc puts his hand on my thigh to try to calm me down. But, unfortunately, it doesn't work this time.

"All three, yes." My voice comes out barely audible as it cracks. I see Luc stiffen beside me, dying to say something.

The officer takes note of what I've said. "Are you able to tell us about these incidents, Ambre? As much detail as you can remember."

The memory of it starts to come back all at once, the feelings, the fear, all of it. Not that it ever entirely went away. It's always been there, haunting me. Drowning me. Making me silently scream for help, but I couldn't. If I did, I'd be dead, and so would my family.

"Ambre, what are you doing at my door?" Eric spits out. I've always hated this man. Something isn't right with him.

"I came to pick up Luc. We're going out." I don't tell him much; he doesn't need to know. It's not like he's Luc's actual father.

"The kid left about five minutes ago. So did Henry. Both went to your place. God knows why."

I turn to leave. I won't stand here a second longer than I have to.

"Okay, bye."

A rough hand reaches out and grabs my arm. "You turned sixteen yesterday, didn't you, barbie doll?"

"Yes." My voice shakes. Why is he touching me?

"Don't you think that deserves celebrating?" His vicious eyes stare into mine, and a corrupt smirk pulls up at his lips.

"I celebrated with my family, yes. Thank you, though. I'm going to go now." I attempt to pull my arm from his grasp. The more I pull, the rougher his grasp becomes. He yanks my arm hard and pulls me close to him, bringing his face inches from mine.

"I didn't get to wish you happy birthday, barbie doll." My heart beats intensely in my chest, my breaths become more rapid. What is he getting at?

"Eric, please let me go home." I look to the floor as tears start to fall from my eyes in fear.

I'm dragged through the front door and thrown on the rough wood floor. What is he doing? I'm sixteen. What could this man possibly want from me? I pray to every God out there that this is just a dream. A vile, vile nightmare. That feels insanely real. Eric slams the door shut. I scurry myself to the corner of the room, hiding as far into the corner as I can. As far away from him as I can be. Eric's tall frame towers over me. Suddenly I'm tugged forward onto the floor, just beneath him. I cower away again. "Barbie doll, if you move away from me one more time, you will regret it. Got it?"

I'm yanked forward once again as he lowers himself just above me. "You want to have some fun?" He spits cruelly as he leaves open-mouthed kisses up my neck.

I shake my head violently. "No, no, no. Let me go, please let me go, please." my voice cracks, and I feel more tears falling down my face. Wriggling does nothing. He's too big. It's useless. I'm trapped. Luc, save me. Luc, save me. Luc, where are you? Luc I need you. My arms are pinned down. He holds both wrists with one hand, gripping hard enough to leave a mark on my wrists. Using all the strength in my body, I kick, I kick where it's going to hurt. Eric inches back and groans in pain. Good.

I use that free second to bolt for the door. I can do this; I can escape. My hand touches the doorknob, and the tension begins to leave my body because I've done it. I've escaped him. Until the hairs on my arms stick up, shivers roll through my entire body, and a heavy breath is on my neck.

"You ever do that again, and you won't leave this room alive. We could have had so much fun together, barbie doll. What a shame."

I don't move. I don't talk. I don't even breathe. Eric has a knife. Looking through the peephole, I see Luc. I see Luc. Luc will save me. I'm going to be okay. Unfortunately, Eric also notices.

His hand comes down to my mouth. "Make a sound, and you'll never see him again."

A sharp pain shoots across my shoulder. I realise what he just did as blood drips down my arm. Not stopping. Not just a drop. Blood pours from my arm; if I don't get that stitched soon, I'll be in trouble. But that was his plan, wasn't it?

"You tripped. You sliced your arm on broken glass. Glass that you broke. Tell anyone anything different, and they won't live to see another day. Tell Luc he won't live to see another day. And neither will you." He lowers the knife and drags it down my body. "Got it? You're lucky your little saviour has shown up. Or you'd be getting a whole lot more." I nod.

Eric wraps an arm around my waist and puts my other arm around his shoulder. Then opens the door in urgency. "Luc! Quick, we need to get her help. She hurt herself whilst waiting for you to get home."

Luc's confused face breaks my heart. I want to tell him everything. I want him to know exactly the type of man he's living with. I don't want Luc or Henry near him ever again. I look at Luc with pleading eyes. I wish he could read my mind. I wish he knew what just happened behind those doors.

"Give her to me. I'll take her to the hospital. Go back inside, Eric."

Eric listens. He played hero. Just like I knew he would.

When we're a far enough distance away from the house, I figure it's safe to talk to Luc, "Hey Luc, can we make sure we always meet at my house and stay away from yours?"

"Yeah, of course, princess. Are you okay? You seem shaken up." He doesn't question why I don't want to be near his house. I don't ask why.

"Eric just makes me feel queasy. That's all."

Luc lets out a small laugh, "Honestly, Eric makes everyone queasy. I understand, don't worry." I smile. I love my best friend so much. I can't ever lose this boy. How can he make me feel so safe after what just happened. And what could have happened if Luc didn't show up.

I explain the events of that day. That day wasn't even the worst of them all. It happened again twice after that. The second time,

I didn't get away. He forced me down, and I was too weak. I couldn't fight him, he forced water down my throat, water that had been tampered with, drugged. I blacked out. When my eyes finally opened, I was in Eric's room, in his bed, and I was covered in blood. I've tried to erase that memory from my mind so many times. I feel dirty, I feel impure, I don't feel at home in my own body.

I don't mention any of this, I'm waiting until Luc isn't here to hear it. I'll let him make his statment, then they can have me back.

My voice was shaking the entire time I spoke to them, my heart was beating rapidly, my head sweating, and my hands clammy. Without realising it, I must have leaned over to Luc. Because I'm now cradled in his arms. And his sleeve is soaked with my tears. The fear still consumes me. I have no proof other than the scar on my shoulder. What if Eric finds out I told people? He'll kill everyone I love.

"I'm sorry; I didn't mean to get emotional." I apologise, wiping my eyes and retreating to my seat. I can't believe I just bawled my eyes out in front of the officer. I bet he doesn't get paid enough for this.

Luc gently turns my head to look at him. He looks empathetically into my eyes, "My princess, never apologise.

Please. You're so freaking strong." And he leaves a gentle kiss on my knuckles, despite the officer still being sat across from us. "Thank you for sharing, Ambre. This will help us a lot. We will ensure that this man is locked up for good. You don't have to live in fear anymore. If you could send in a photo of this scar, that would also help a lot. You may leave the room now. Luc will be out shortly." I don't want to be alone right now. But I listen. I give Luc a small smile and leave the room.

Chapter 19 🗼

Luc

After talking to the officer, I finally get a minute to process. Eric not only abused me for years and nearly took my life, but he also sexually assaulted my Ambre. And threatened to kill her if she told anyone. I can't believe she had to go through that alone. She was *sixteen*. If she had told me, I would have killed him myself. It's taking all of my self-control right now. All I want is to find Eric and make him pay for what he's done. But I guess that's what the whole prison thing is for. He deserves to suffer more. I need to find Ambre. I know she will not want to be alone right now. How has she managed to keep this to herself for so long and still be her usual bubbly self? God, no wonder she didn't want a relationship to ruin us. If she lost me, she'd feel more alone than ever; she needed me to keep her safe and make her feel comforted, not to kiss her. I know that's forgotten now, but I'm realising now more than ever just how stupid I was and why she reacted the way she did.

I make my way over to the park, where we decide to meet afterwards. The second Ambre comes into view, I run over to her and pull her gently into my arms. "You're *so* strong, princess. I'm so God damn proud of you," I whisper into her ear. As I pull away, I hold onto both of her hands and look into her watery eyes. "Ambre, I promise you will never go through anything alone ever again." I feel my eyes begin to water, but I hold them back. One of us has to be strong right now, and she's been strong for too long.

This beautiful girl is my world. My best friend. My favourite person on this planet.

"I'm sorry I didn't tell you. He said he'd kill you if I did." As much as she's trying to hold back the tears for everyone else's sake, they escape anyway. I wipe away a tear with my thumb. I pull her close to me, into my arms, away from everyone, "Baby, you don't have to be sorry for anything. You are the strongest person I know. You're safe now. You're always going to be safe with me. I promise." She nods as she wipes the tears away with her sleeve. She cuddles in closer to me, and I hold her for as long as she needs.

I catch Caroline up on everything, as Ambre asked me to. Caroline let out many angry words about Eric. As did I.

It's new years eve. One of my favourite days. Spending it with
people I don't hate, some that are like my family, and everything
feels normal. The annual new years eve party that friends and
family come to. It's amazing. And every year on this very night, I
get to kiss Ambre, no weird, awkward aftermath. Just a kiss, as
friends, of course. The girls spend the day clothes shopping; I
wear my usual pants, white shirt and tie, I decorate the house,
and the girls come home with even more decorations. It's special
to me anyway.

Ambre

The other day was hard. Harder for Luc. I know he's gone
through so much more. I probably overreacted to the whole
thing; it was just hard to tell people. But that's over now. Today
is a good day. It will be amazing. Nothing will ruin today for us.
Ami, Care, and I are going shopping for dresses. Henry is
cooking with my Mum. We love dress shopping. There's this one
dress I saw a while ago that I'm dying to wear. It's silver, sparkly,
and will definitely make me look like a sexy disco ball. It's *perfect*.
I know Ami is looking forward to seeing her Dad later. She sees

him a couple of times a month, I know she wants to see him more, but she's an angel and takes what time she can get with him.

Amélie's Dad is the last guy my Mum dated. They were in love. They were engaged. Then he packs up and leaves for LA for a job. They both knew that we couldn't up route our lives to live in LA. Amélie and I grew up here; this is our home. This is my Mums home. Not to mention how expensive that would be. There wasn't anyways for us to afford that. So they decided the long distance wasn't going to work. So he comes and visits a couple of times a month. Flies over and gets a hotel for two nights tops. I wish he was around more for Ami; she adores him. He's a movie producer now. Ami aspires to be an actress because of the movies he's produced. He isn't a bad man, I guess he does what he can, but he could have done more. He could have been there more.

He's been there a whole lot more than my Dad, though. My Dad left when I was born. As I grew older, I noticed his absence more, I questioned it, and I forced my Mum to give me his number. Every day I would message him, every day I called. And every day, he ignored me. I pleaded for him to just be a Dad. All I wanted was love. I wanted a text every once in a while. I wanted him to love me like his daughter, not ignore me like I'm a stranger.

A young girl needs her father there, and he never was. So I eventually gave up on him. I tried forgetting about him, putting him in the back of my mind. It's always there, though. The thoughts run through my head when all is quiet. Questions like *why? Wasn't I good enough? Is it me?* I'll get over it one day, I'm sure. I just need closure.

Party time! I got the dress. Ami is wearing her *slightly* small red dress. Care has a satin forest green dress and looks model-worthy wearing it. Henry wears an adorable tux, and I do indeed look like a sexy disco ball. Before heading downstairs, I apply an extra layer of concealer to my scar. I've always done this to stop questions. Luc always assumed it was from my "fall", but I'm still the world's worst liar. So I don't put myself in the position where I'd need to lie to anyone.

There's a light knock at my bedroom door. As I open it, I'm greeted by a very handsome-looking Luc, with purple tulips in his hand.

"For you, m'lady." He leans in and picks up my hand to kiss my knuckles.

"Why, thank you, kind sir," I say, taking the tulips from his hands and giving him a curtsy.

"Shall we?" He asks, extending an arm.

"We shall." I smile widely at him. *My boy.*

When we reach the living room, everyone is already here with a drink in their hand. We walk over to Amélie, Henry, and Care and see they also have drinks in their hands.

"Woah, Woah, I'm going to need to see some ID, Miss Amélie and Mr Henry." Henry freezes for a second, but Ami just nudges him and laughs. *My family.*

I pull at Luc's arm, "Hey, I'm going to go get a drink from the kitchen. Want something?"

"Just a water for now, please; I'll save the good stuff for later." He says with a wink. I smile and shake my head.

Getting closer to the kitchen, I hear one familiar voice and another voice I can't quite decipher. My Mum and- *who is that?* They aren't talking. They're screaming. I don't enter the kitchen yet; I stand by the doorway and listen, keeping hidden.

"Joshua, you need to leave! What will you say to Ambre? You can't be here." Joshua?

"I have the right to see her! She is my daughter just as much as yours."

My daughter? Wait, Joshua is my father? My father is here? Right now, standing in my kitchen is my father. The man who left me eighteen years ago, not a single message in that eighteen years, except a mere 'Stop contacting this number.'

"No, Joshua. You stopped having the right to call *my girl* your daughter the second you walked out on us. She stopped being your daughter each time you ignored her calls, each time you broke her heart. Now leave my home."

"I'm not going anywhere until I see my daughter."

"She does not want to see you! She doesn't need you screwing with her head. Not today, not tonight, not ever, Joshua! Now please, go."

I walk in slowly and stare at him in disbelief. It's him. It's really him. I've seen photos, but that's all. His back is turned to me, so he doesn't know I'm here yet. That is until he sees the expression on my Mums face.

"Oh, Hunny. Please go back to the lounge."

"Dad? Is it really you?" I audibly swallow. I don't know if I'm ready.

"It's me, Ambs. I'm here, sweetie." My mouth opens in shock. In disbelief. Did he just call me *sweetie?*

"*Sweetie?* I'm not even going to give you the satisfaction of calling you Dad once more. What are you doing here? You've had no problem staying away for the past eighteen years."

"I want to be a part of your life." He looks serious. And not at all guilty.

"Yeah? Well, I'm sorry to tell you this, but you're *years* too late. I'm an adult next month. You can't show up eighteen years later and expect me to be fine with this." I try to keep my composure, but my emotions win. How can he make me feel so worthless and stupid for my entire childhood? How could he abandon me and suddenly show up now?

"Don't be like that. Come on! I'm here now."

"You're here now? What and that's supposed to be good enough for me? That's supposed to compensate for the years of heartbreak and pain you gave me? I don't think so."

"I'm sorry."

"Is sorry meant to make up for everything? God, you're meant to be my Dad. You're meant to protect me, make me feel so loved, make me feel like no boy will ever be good enough for me. Instead, you made me feel like I'll never be good enough for *anyone*. I mean, how can anyone love me if my own father doesn't, right? You broke my heart before any boy ever could."

"I want to make up for all of that now. You're my daughter, and I want to be a part of your life, Ambre."

"There is one thing I know for sure, Joshua, was it? I sure as hell am not your daughter. You don't have the right to walk into my life eighteen years later and act like you've been there all along. I pleaded. I begged you to want me, but you didn't want to. I begged you to send a text once a day. Was that too much to ask? Do you know how hard it is for a little girl to try and even comprehend why her Dad doesn't want her? I've been dying to say all this, and so much more the second I realised how much of a dirtbag you really are and how I don't need you in my life. I needed my father, but you? You are not my father. And I'm so glad that I know that now." I don't realise how much I've said in so little time until I see his open-mouthed expression.

"I don't need you. Not anymore. Leave, and don't come back."

"I don't want to leave." He's doing the thing my Mum always said he was good at. He's trying to guilt-trip me. He's trying to *manipulate* me. He looks down and messes with his hands; it looks forced, and it seems like an act.

"Funny, you had no problem leaving a little girl with no father. I'm sure you'll survive this time around as well. Buh-bye." Mum pushes his back until he's out the door.

I can't believe that just happened. I just met my father. I told him everything I'd written in my diary since I learned to write. Everything I needed to say. Now he's gone. *I feel like I've had my closure.*

I walk over to my Mum and put my head on her shoulder. Only then do I let myself cry. There was no way in hell I was allowing that man to see me break. "Hunny, you did so well. My brave girl. You told him off better than I ever could have. I'm so proud of you." She says in her comforting voice and leaves a kiss on my forehead. "Go fix your makeup now, beautiful. No tears on new years." She gives me a soft smile. I nod and head upstairs.

I dab at the smudged mascara and re-apply it tidily. As I go to sit down for a second, my door is opened.

"Hey, Ambs. I saw you come up here. Everything okay?" Care.

"I'm okay, Care. It's just that somebody showed up. Somebody, I didn't think I'd ever see."

"Your Dad?" She asks softly whilst putting her arm around me.

"Yeah." I give a weak smile and lean into her.

"Forget about him, babe. Let's go have the best night ever. We'll eat too much, drink *way* too much, and kiss some hot guy when the clock hits midnight. Sound good?"

I let out a small laugh. "Yeah, sounds good."

"Come on then, beautiful. Don't let him dull your shine. Especially not tonight." And we head back down to the party.

Chapter 20

Ambre

The music is blasting. I can barely hear myself think. It's perfect.
I search through the crowd of people for Luc, Ami and Henry.
There are a lot more people here this year. I swear this thing
never used to have so many people. How our house can throw
such a huge party is beyond me. I catch a glimpse of Luc and
make my way over that way. Care goes off to find Ami.

"Luc! I've been searching for you. Where's Ami?" I shout over
the music.

"Henry wasn't feeling like partying right now, so they've headed
up to Amélie's room for now. Where have you been? I've been
sat here looking all lonely for twenty minutes." He says with a
pout.

"A lot has happened in the past twenty minutes that you're
going to need filling in on later, though. So let's just have fun
and bring in the new year with smiles."

"Okay, princess. Whatever you say." He says into my ear and leaves a small kiss on my cheek. It was such a small gesture which probably didn't mean anything, yet it meant too much to me. "Are you feeling okay? You're all red. Have you got a temperature?" He puts his hand on my forehead; great. I was clearly blushing.

I wack his hand away, "Luc, I'm good. Honestly, I'm fine. It's just warm, that's all."

"Hm, okay. If you say so." He eyes me suspiciously. "It is quite warm, though; let's go outside." He grabs my hand and pulls me along with him.

"Wait, the countdown! It's five minutes to midnight. It'll start soon."

"We'll hear it from outside. Plus, this way, we get to watch the fireworks go off. How romance novel worthy." He adds with a wink. I give him a light nudge and smile.

From where we live, we can see the fireworks go off near the big ben clock. It's phenomenal actually. We usually stay inside and celebrate with everyone else. This year I'd rather it be just Luc and I. I think I need this time with my best friend, not with a group of people.

Luc and I set up a blanket on the floor underneath the magnolia tree, which lives in the small park across from my house. I spent most of my childhood in this little park, sitting under this exact tree with a blanket and a book. This tree always made me feel like I'm living in a book-worthy fantasy world; it's so bewitching, you look up, and it's as if you're sitting in an enchanted forest. It's beautiful. It's most certainly the best place to watch fireworks and bring in the new year perfectly.

From a distance, we hear the shouts begin. I snuggle in close to Luc; it's freezing. We look at one another and smile. We exchange a knowing look. The look that says 'we did it' we survived yet another year, and it has been a hard one. Here we are, together, despite having nearly lost our friendship. And despite every challenge life has thrown our way. We made it. Ambre and Luc, *always*.

"Ten! Nine! Eight!" I glance at Luc. We smile widely and yell out the countdown together. I look up at the sky; it's clear. It's December thirty-first, and the sky is clear. It's a miracle. The stars light the whole sky and make this whole night seem even more surreal. "Three, two, one-"

Luc dips his head and leaves a soft kiss on my lips as fireworks shoot in the air, leaving rays of colour in the sky. "Happy new

year, princess. We're going to take on the world, you and me."
With that, he leaves a peck on my forehead.

Luc and I have always been each other's new year's kiss, but we usually kiss each other on the cheek. I'm glad he broke that tradition this year.

"Happy new year, my Luc." I can't stop the smile from spreading across my face. I wrap my arms around him and cuddle in closer as we watch the firework display. "It's going to be a good year; I can feel it."

Luc looks down and smiles at me purely. "Yes, princess, it is."

Nothing has changed between us. But I can't help feeling like it has.

Chapter 21

Luc

Home day. Caroline and I have tickets to fly back at four am today. Ambre has tickets to fly back at seven pm tonight. I have to sit next to Caroline on a plane and try my very best to not jump out of the plane parachuteless. It's going to be a challenge. What do you talk to a girl like Caroline about for a whole hour? Coffee? Her only personality trait is being addicted to coffee. I wish Ambre was getting the same flight as us, but she's spending the day having one last 'eat junk food until you feel sick whilst watching movies' day. *Her* words. Apparently, it's absolutely mandatory that they do that before Ambre returns to Paris. We were invited to join. Unfortunately, I didn't plan to stay in London for an extra day to eat food and watch movies, so I already booked the tickets.

Goodbye London, hello Paris.

"What is your opinion on planes? Do you like planes? Are you one of those people who have to be by the window?" Caroline goes on for about ten minutes, non-stop talking.

"Caroline, for the love of God, shut up. How do you have this much energy at four am? Please enlighten me."

"Coffee."

"Yep. Why did I even ask?" I put my head in my hands. I'm too tired for this. We were meant to be on the plane half an hour ago.

"Because you're not thinking straight yet. You know why?"

"No, Caroline, I don't. But I'm sure you're going to tell me."

"It's because you have not had coffee, and I have."

"Thank you. Thank you so much for that useful piece of information."

"Shush! I think we're boarding." She jumps to her feet and scans the doors as if she has x-ray vision and can see what's going on behind them.

"Caroline, there's nobody there yet; we are not-" I stop talking when I see the doors open, and everyone starts boarding. Caroline looks back at me with a smug smile. Now she can add gloating to the list of things to annoy me with, perfect. "Sorry, what was that you were saying? Because I believe we are, in fact, boarding now."

"I can see that. Thank you, Caroline."

"Luc! Seriously, why do you have to say my full name in every sentence? Can't you just call me Care as most normal people do? Sorry, I forgot you weren't normal; you're boring." She rolls her eyes dramatically at me, and I thought Ambre was dramatic. I feel bad for the poor soul who gets stuck with Caroline.

"You see, to call you *Care* would insinuate that I actually *care* about you, which I don't."

"Oh no, you definitely do. We are going to be besties, and you know it." She slings an arm around my shoulder as we stand in this ridiculously long line.

I gently remove her arm and place it back at her side. "No, we're not. Trust me."

"Luc, you bought me a plane ticket to London and back. I *think* that means you care."

"It doesn't," I say sternly. I'm beginning to regret my decision to buy the said ticket.

"Er, it kind of does." She proceeds to whine. I should've bought earplugs. How am I going to survive an hour in such close proximity to this girl?

"I got you tickets to surprise Ambre. To make her happy."

"Speaking of Ambre, has anything happened with you two yet?"
She's smirking. Why is she smirking?

"No. Stop smirking; you're creeping me out."

"Good, it's meant to creep you out. So nothing happened?" She
asks with her voice in a significantly higher pitch.

"No, Caroline. Nothing happened. What do you know?" I look
in any direction that is not her eyes. She's staring into my soul
with those emerald eyes.

"What do you think I know?" She asks as she jumps with
excitement. Was it excitement? I can't tell with this girl.

"Jeez, Caroline. Just spit it out, whatever you so desperately
want to annoy me about."

"I saw you kiss. And I thought you might want to keep this
moment forever, so-"

"Caroline, please tell me you did not take a picture," I say
exasperated.

"I took a picture." She squeals and instantly pulls her phone out.

"Of course you did," I say more to myself because is she
listening? No. Is she ever actually listening? No.

As it turns out, the plane is what saves me! As we finally reach
the front of the queue, Caroline is forced to shut up and pull
out our boarding passes. Hallelujah.

This is going to be one painful journey.

Home. Well, it will be once Ambre gets home. I put the key in the front door; however, it's already unlocked-

I put the key between my fingers, I learnt that one from Ambre. She says it's what she does when she's alone or feels unsafe at any point. I *hate* that she ever has to feel unsafe.

Slowly, I creak open the door. It smells like lavender. Why does it smell like lavender? What is this robber doing, testing every incent before stealing them?

"Surprise!" A voice beams behind me. Before I can register what or who it was, my fist flies at the thing closest to me and hits something, well, someone.

I squeeze my eyes shut; I'm scared to open them. Who did I just hit? "I am so sorry. I didn't mean to hurt anyone unless you're a robber. Then I definitely meant to hurt you."

A pained sound leaves someone's mouth before replying, "It's okay, don't worry. Blood is dripping from my nose, but I'll be alright." *Alexandre.*

"Alexandre, would you care to explain what you're doing in my apartment, scaring the life out of me?" I say sharply. I can still feel my pulse beating erratically.

"Luc, seriously, what is with you and being unable to use a nickname? I'm *Alex*. Notice how people don't say the andre? I'm assuming Luc is short for Lucas, right? So why don't I start calling you Lucas?" He spits out impatiently. What has gotten into him? "And for future reference, when somebody shouts 'surprise' it usually means they were trying to surprise you. Isn't that crazy?" The sarcasm drips from his voice.

"And what has gotten into you? It's never been an issue before. Also, never call me Lucas again, got it?" Nobody calls me Lucas. My Mam named me Lucas because it's a french name and she was french. However, everyone, including her, has always called me Luc. Only Eric called me Lucas.

"Maybe I just got fed up with you calling me something I don't like being called. Clearly, you know the feeling. I know you've got something against me; it's quite obvious, by the way. I just don't know what. I've always treated you the same as everyone else as if you had been here all along."

I run my hand down my face. How do I reply to that? I'm not a people person. I can barely cope with Caroline. I force myself to keep quiet and not snap *every time* I'm near her. I wasn't so fond of him when he was flirting with Ambre all the time, either. But he doesn't need to know that.

"You're not wrong, *Alex*. Maybe I've been slightly harsh on you. I'm sorry." I spit out quickly. I hated that.

"Wow. That was really hard for you, wasn't it?" He studies me with an amused look on his face. Great, another person with something to hold against me. "Thank you for your apology. Just call me Alex and say 'hey' once in a while. It's not hard, man." I nod stiffly. This isn't a fun conversation.

How long does an all-day movie marathon last day? Ah, right. All freaking day. I need Ambre to get on that plane *now* and be here *now*.

The door creaks open, and Lucie walks in. I look the opposite way. I haven't got a word I'd like to say to her. She's the reason Ambre, and I was apart for so long. If she had given me that letter as Ambre planned, we would have spoken and returned to each other much faster.

"Hey, Luc. Good trip?" Lucie asks cautiously.

"Lucie, I'm not interested in small talk with you." She looks down with a slight nod. Alex moves closer to her and wraps his arm around her waist as if it were the most natural thing on earth. What is going on there? That's new.

"None of that went to plan, but the original plan was to come here, make it look and smell nice for you and Ambre, set up some games and have a game night. Sound okay?" Alex cuts in.

"Ambre is going to be exhausted when she gets home. She'll be full of jet lag; maybe it's best you go home. Sorry." I say full of "sympathy" I'm not sorry at all. I want them to go home. I want to spend the night talking and spending time with Ambre. With *just* Ambre.

"Luc, she's flying from London. We're one hour ahead. You know that, right? If you don't know that, how the hell did you get into this university?" He looks serious for a second until he exaggeratingly lifts his hand to his chin and starts doing a ridiculous thinking pose. I can't *wait* for this one. "Wait, you seduced the chancellor, didn't you?" Alex says, full of pride.

"Ha ha, so funny."

"A for effort, Luc. If you don't want us here that much, we can go. We just thought it'd be nice to get the whole group together; Lucie and I have news we want to share with everyone."

"Is the news that you're dating? Trust me, it won't be news the second they see you. You're not subtle. Work on it."

Lucie moves her hand over her mouth in an attempt to hide a prideful smile? Happy smile? She's smiling, and I don't know why. But she's trying to hide it and failing.

"You're good," Alex smiles and points at me stupidly. Whatever little act they're playing, they suck. "Have you considered taking law instead of fir-" Lucie hits his arm in a rush. *She told him.* I told her nobody is to know I'm taking that class. I want to surprise Ambre. If Alex has known for a while, I guarantee Ambre knows as well. Unless he's been told recently.

"Lucie, you told him? I told you to keep that quiet."

"I'm sorry. I can't hide things from people I'm close to!"

"There was no reason for him to know. If it was something about you, sure tell him. It wasn't for you to tell people. There's a reason I want that quiet." I turn to Alex and give him a pleading look, "Alex, please tell me Ambre doesn't know."

He puts his hands up, "If she does, it's not from me. I've not told a soul." I nod. I need these people to leave now. I've had enough social interaction with people that aren't Ambre for one day.

"Luc, this probably isn't the best time-"

I cut her off quickly, "Lucie, if it isn't the best time, save it for a better time. I'm stressed enough as it is."

"Please. It'll take two minutes." I look at her with a waiting look.

"Oh, okay. So to start, I'm sorry. *I'm so so sorry.* When Ambre handed me the letter and flowers I should have given them to you the second you walked through the door. I know that. I guess I thought if you read the letter, you'd want her to come back, and you'd kick me away. I was scared of being left. I really am sorry. Please forgive me, Luc. I'll also apologise to Ambre as soon as I see her as well."

"What you did was messed up. You made a mistake. I hate what you did, but I don't hate you. I know you've dealt with some stuff which might cause you to act that way, so I'm hearing you out. I won't hold it against you. Now your challenge is to get Ambre to forgive you. Tonight isn't the smartest idea; she'll be home late and cranky from eating too much. Try Ambre tomorrow." I pause for a second, thinking if I should ask them to leave so Ambre and I can spend time together alone or have them stay for a game night.

Apparently, I don't need to make that decision; Alex takes over for me. "As much as I really would love to spend the night playing board games and drinking, I can tell you want to be alone. I'm sure you're exhausted from dealing with Care's non-stop talking for an hour straight. Don't worry, you'll get used to her."

"Woah, drinking? Never mind, I'm in." I joke. I'm trying this new thing called not hating everyone. It's already exhausting.

They both laugh. Alex takes hold of Lucie's hand, and they make their way out. "Goodbye, Luc." I lift a hand in goodbye. *Alone at last.* Great, now I miss Ambre even more.

Chapter 22 🗼

Ambre

I'm home. I step out of the taxi into the cold French night. The wind is strong, and the rain is heavy. It's perfect. I love winter. What isn't there to love about winter? There's Christmas music, hot chocolate with marshmallows, wrapping up in cute jumpers and scarves, snow and rain, and candles in the dark whilst watching movies. It's all even better when you're doing it with your best friend.

The past few weeks have been hectic, to say the least. And now everything can go back to normal. This is all my normal now: waking up at ridiculous times and running on caffeine, going to class, reading books by the Eiffel tower. It's the best normal I've ever had. I mean, it's been my dream since I was younger. I always knew what I wanted. This is what I wanted. To study in Paris, to live with my best friend, to have a fat cat as my furry companion, to become a writer. I've made it all come true. Determination pays off. I truly believe that if you want something enough, you *can* make it happen. And nothing can get in your way. I'm still working on becoming a writer. I've been writing a book for a while now. I planned and prepared, I wrote drafts, and I changed them. It's all a part of it. I'm so excited to be able to say it's nearly finished. *Dreams come true.* Honestly, I think I owe my love of France to my Mum. She and Luc's Mam grew up in Paris; this was their home. They were roommates just as Luc and I are now. That is why we have French names despite growing up in London. The same goes for Amélie and Henry.

As I open the door to the apartment, I'm hit with the smell of candles. Walking into a warm apartment lit by candles on a rainy winter's night, does it get better than that? Yes, it does. I'm walking into a warm apartment to my cuddly best friend waiting for me on the couch with blankets and hot chocolate. I adore this boy.

I drop my suitcase and let Chubbs out of his carrier and run over to Luc. I throw myself on top of him and cuddle into him. "I've missed you."

"I've missed you more, princess. I hope you're not too tired. I have a surprise for you later."

"Later? It's like nine pm. How can you have a surprise for later?" I ask suspiciously. What has he got planned?

"You'll see, and you'll love it. I promise." He says, looking at me sincerely.

"Okay, I trust you. What time is this surprise happening? I want to cuddle up to Chubbs in bed and sleep."

"Ambre, that's what you want to do every day. It's at one am." He says the last part cautiously because he knows I like my sleep. I don't want to go out at one am!

"*One* am? What? What could you possibly have planned? Wait, I know. You want to take me out in the dark, so nobody will see you murder me, right? Classic horror movie."

He smiles and rolls his eyes. "Yes, Ambre, that is definitely my plan. If I had been planning on killing you, don't you think I would have done it already?" He says sarcastically whilst giving me a playful look.

"Who knows, maybe you're playing the long game."

"I don't have that type of patience, and you know it."

"That is very true. Okay, you're off the hook." I laugh.

Sarcastically he responds, "Oh, am I? Thanks, I appreciate that." Then smiles at me and shakes his head. "You're a piece of work."

"You love it."

"C'mere." He says before pulling me into him and cuddling me tight. "Let's start a new series. We have some time to pass anyway."

"Sure." I grab the remote and begin scrolling through different films. "Hm, this one looks good. 'Romance set in Italy. Two friends move abroad to study in a new country but get tangled up in new feelings as they explore this romantic setting and see each other in a new light....' That one sounds good!" I click play; there is no way we're not watching this.

"It sounds like an Ambre series."

"No, it sounds like an Ambre and Luc series." I say excitedly.

He smiles down at me, "Whatever you say, princess."

We're halfway into the first episode before Luc starts commenting on things. Every damn time. "Come on, that's not realistic. You don't move somewhere new and suddenly fall in love with your best friend."

"Luc, it's not meant to be realistic! There's a reason it's called fiction. It's made for people like me who don't want to live in the real world." He's quiet for the rest of that episode. But as soon as we start the next...

"Did they seriously just kiss? Already? It's the second episode. Maybe they are in love, but how has it happened that fast?

Surely they need to try the whole convince themselves it'll ruin everything, hide your feelings, protect your heart, right?"

"Wow, sounding real experience there. Have you seen this before?" I say sarcastically while laughing. "Luc, this isn't a slow burn. We love slow burns, but sometimes you just need the romance from beginning to end. Sometimes you can't wait for it. You know?"

"Yeah, I get what you mean." He replies casually, but his saddened face is a whole different tone.

"Hey, are you okay? If this is upsetting you, we can turn it off."

"No, I'm actually quite enjoying it. I'm just thinking, don't worry."

"Well, stop thinking. It's not good for you." I joke.

Halfway into the second episode, they start confessing how they've always loved each other. It's adorable. I swear I even see a real hint of interest on Luc's face. "See, how romantic is this? Friends to lovers is superior."

"Yes, it is, princess." He says, placing a soft kiss on my forehead.

"Keep your eyes closed." Luc says whilst guiding me.

"I couldn't see if my eyes were open. Your hand is covering my eyes and my nose! Move your hand. I can't breathe properly." I exaggerate.

"Right yeah, sorry. Okay, we're here. Keep your eyes closed." He lowers me onto what feels like grassy ground, covered by a blanket. I sit down and wait for the instructions to open my eyes. Luc sits next to me and puts his arm around my shoulder, keeping me warm. "One more minute." I rub my hands impatiently. I want to know why my eyes are closed! "Ready?"

"Always." I say smiling

I slowly open my eyes, and my mouth drops. The Eiffel tower is nothing but sparkles. It's the most ethereal thing I've ever seen. I feel a tear roll down my cheek. *I'm living a fantasy.* "Luc, I don't know what to say. It's phenomenal. It's everything I dreamed it would be and more."

"I'm so glad, princess."

Luc

Ambre has been through a lot. Especially the past few weeks. I figured she might need something to take her away from reality for a while. I knew this would do it. This has always been a fantasy of Ambre's. She told me when we were tiny. She wants to see the Eiffel tower sparkle. I knew from that day that I would make her dream come true. Her dream would come true, and I'd experience it with her. The look on her face makes staying up until one am worth it. She's so captured in this moment. Her eyes are glimmering; she looks like she's in heaven. Her expression of adoration and pure happiness makes my heart melt.

"My heart is smiling right now. You made my heart beam, Luc Bonet." Her eyes glisten with tears of happiness. Her dreams are coming true. And I'm a part of it.

"Ambre de Roselle, I want nothing more than to make your heart smile every hour of the day." She grins at me and throws her arms around me, bringing me into a tight embrace.

"I have a new dream." She looks up at me giddily.

"Let's make it come true." I take her in, everything about her in this moment. How her dimples pop out from her constant smile. How her eyes shimmer looking at the Eiffel tower. If you pay close enough attention, you can see the pure wonder-struck in her expression.

"I want to be proposed to here, next to the Eiffel tower as it sparkles. That's my new dream." I make a mental note, you know to tell her future fiancé. "I want to stand right here remembering this moment with déjà vu. I want to remember the first time my heart smiled so much it hurt. It's all because of you, Luc."

Now my heart's smiling. Watching this girl so *encaptured* by the Eiffel tower and purely loving every second of this moment.

Suddenly it hits me. I'm so truly in love with this girl with every fibre of my being.

Screw her *'future fiancé'*. I'm going to be the one to make her dream come true.

"Let's go for a swim." I suggest as we're walking past the river Seine.

"Very funny. Where do you suggest we swim? In the freezing cold river Seine? I think not."

"Come on. It'll be fun. Nobody is around. It's just us."

"I can't. What will I wear? I'm not getting my dress wet because I'll have to walk home absolutely freezing."

"You can wear my t-shirt. Please. We made your dream come true tonight. So let's make mine come true."

"This is a dream of yours? You never told me." She asks with a guilty look on her face. "I can't believe I didn't know this was your dream. I'm sorry." It's not her fault she didn't know. I've never told anyone. I keep my dreams to myself. Rather than tell people my plans, I show them my results. Ambre is the opposite. She's always been one to think out loud. To plan her entire life and tell me every detail. I love that about her. I love *her*.

"I never told anyone, princess. I'm telling you now because I want you to be the one I make this dream come true with."

"Deal."

I kiss Ambre's cheek, sprint towards the river, and dive in.

Ambre

"Luc! You forgot to give me your shirt!" I yell, running after him.

A big splash is all I hear as a response. I sit on the ledge, waiting for Luc to come up. Seconds later, his head pops up. "What was that, princess?"

"Your shirt." I laugh.

Luc swims over to me and pulls himself out of the river. He inches toward me and will soak me with a hug. I know that's what he's trying to do. I back away so he can't reach me. "Come on, give me a hug." He laughs as he runs around after me.

"Luc, go away," I say between giggles. I carry on running until a pair of arms wrap around my waist and lift me off the ground. I squeal and attempt to wriggle from his grasp, but it's too late. I'm already soaked. "I can not believe you just did that. I'm drenched! You're annoying." I stick my bottom lip out before laughing.

"You love me, really." He winks whilst stripping off his dripping wet shirt and then putting it in my hands.

Oh. *Oh.*

Where has Luc been hiding this body? *Wow.*

"Are you going to pick your jaw up off the floor, or shall I do that for you?" He jokes.

"Oh, shut up. My jaw was not on the floor. Don't flatter yourself." I try to stop myself from checking him out as I say this because, *wow.*

"You sure? Because I think you've got some drool dripping there as well." He jokes and rubs his thumb down my lip.

"You wish." I say confidently. Best to keep composure, that is, until I totally freak out over what I see going up Luc's back to his shoulder. "Oh my, God. Your tattoo."

"You like it?"

"I love it." I answer genuinely. I trace the flames up his back; they're exquisite. The tattoo artist really did a good job. The tattoo isn't coloured, but I think black and white gives it a better impact. "Luc, it's beautiful. Is it for your Dad?" I question.

"Yeah, it is."

"It's perfect." I say, placing a kiss on his shoulder. His shoulder that I have to tip-toe to reach. "You jump into the river and keep your back turned. I'm going to change into your shirt."

"Got it." And he's gone with a splash.

I was nervous about wearing this at; first; I wasn't sure how much it would cover. To my luck, it reaches just above my knees. I run at full speed towards the river, feeling the wind behind me, tiny droplets of rain fall onto my face, and the grass between my toes, feeling *alive*. "Here goes nothing," I whisper as I leap into the water and land with a splash.

I come up for air and notice that the rain has gotten heavier within the three seconds I'd gone underwater. It will be chucking it down with rain in the next five minutes. I search for Luc and jump onto his back when I see him.

"Hey," I say with a smile.

"Hello there, princess. He grins. How does it fit?"

"Perfectly. Also, I thought you should know it's going to be heavy rain very soon."

"All the more fun."

"Aren't you freezing?" I question him as if he were crazy. Because he is.

"I am. But you feeling comfortable is more important to me." I stare down at him from his back in adoration. He's my world. As I said, rain is pouring from the sky within seconds. I've experienced many rainy days and nights in Paris, but this is by far the most magical one.

"Is it safe for us to be in here whilst it rains?" I question.

"I'm not sure. But you only live once, right?" I give him a stern look. "I wouldn't ever let anything happen to you, Ambre. I promise."

"I believe you." I jump down off his back and swim around to face him.

"You're perfect in every single way, Ambre." He says, holding onto both of my hands. "Did you know that your smile is so beautiful it could light up the entirety of Paris?"

I stare at him in wonder, "I didn't know that. But thank you for informing me."

I smile up at him. Rain pours down onto us; it's dripping down Luc's face, soaking his hair to the point that droplets fall off his hair onto his face.

Luc stares into my eyes intently, and I stare back. I notice his eyes dip down to my lips and back up quickly. "Ambre,"

"Luc,"

"I'm so in love with you it hurts." He says, lowering his lips to mine. I taste the raindrops on his lips. I wrap my arms around his neck and pull myself up onto his waist. Luc deepens the kiss whilst the rain continues to pour down on us. Now, this is a romance novel-worthy kiss. He tucks my soaking locks behind my ears and continues to kiss me. I don't break it apart. Instead, I run my hand up his chest, taking every second of this moment. Luc breaks the kiss slowly. "I'm sorry, I had to tell you. It was killing me. It kills me just being around you, seeing you every day, and not being able to tell you how I'm really feeling."

"Luc, never apologise for being honest with me. Never." I kiss him softly on his lips. "I wish I knew what to say."

"You don't have to say you love me too. I sprung it on you. I kind of sprung it on myself, to be honest. I just had to tell you."

"I think I need time. Just some time to think about everything. I'm having trouble trying to decipher my feelings."

"You can think out loud with me if you want. Maybe I can help." He looks at me with a pleading look in his eyes.

"I love you so freaking much. But am I *in* love? I don't know. What if I mistake one for the other?"

"Princess, when you know, you'll know. It'll hit you out of nowhere. And you'll suddenly question, how have I been denying myself of this feeling for so long? That's how I felt when I saw you gawking at the Eiffel tower. Completely mesmerised by sparkles. That's when I realised I'm so completely, irrevocably in love with you, Ambre de Roselle. I'm in so deep, and I never want to come to the surface again."

I kiss his lips again slowly, intently, giving him all the love I have in the small gesture. I rest my forehead against Luc's and smile. "Luc Bonet, you really are incredible."

Chapter 23

Luc

Tomorrow is Ambre's birthday. So today, I'm spending the day at the art studio, finishing her gift. A small group of people go all the time. I've actually grown to like a few of them.

Ambre has so many classes today, and she's got to stay late in English lit to discuss an upcoming trip. Something about a wilderness trip so they can write poems about it. But Ambre has asked me to bring Chubbs to the studio today. According to her, Chubbs has separation anxiety and has to be with one of us at all times. So I have been given the job of cat-sitter. Nobody will mind, though. Believe it or not, many people bring pets. Last week somebody brought their pet ferret in. Chubbs won't cause any harm; all he does is sleep. And that's exactly how he became Chubbs.

Finishing this piece is going to feel amazing. Seeing Ambre's reaction will feel even better. I'm not going to lie; I wish she had said she was also in love with me yesterday. But I'll wait for as long as she needs. I'm not going anywhere. Because I'm going to be the one to make her dream of being proposed to by the Eiffel tower come true. Nobody else, me.

"Have fun at the art studio today! I'm sure your little besties have missed you." She jokes. "I'm already late to class and still need caffeine, so I'm going to run. Bye!" And she's gone.

I walk into the studio, and I'm hit with the scent of paint and oils. I can't imagine a better smell to be welcomed with.

"Luc, it's wonderful to have you back. And who's this chubby little fella?" Vivienne says as she strokes Chubbs and gets purrs out of him. Vivienne owns this place, and she adores cats. So we call her Viv for short. It's easier.

"He's exactly that. His name is Chubbs." Viv laughs.

"Well, that's a wonderful name. My husband and I have a cat who looks very similar to Chubbs. I'm sure they'd get along swell." She says, retreating back to the painting area.

"Sure they would." I agree with her; it's easier to agree than try to convince her otherwise. I follow her through to the painting area and head straight to the easel I usually work at. Viv walks over with my painting in hand.

"It looks amazing, Luc. Ambre is going to love it." I smile at her appreciatively.

I started working on a bigger canvas about a month ago. I figured my sketching paper just wouldn't do it. After Christmas, I've got all the more to add to it. I need this to be perfect by the end of today. I'll spend the entire day here if necessary. "Here, let me take Chubbs over to the pet sanctuary." She says, grabbing Chubbs. I wouldn't have a clue if somebody asked me what a pet sanctuary was. Viv tends to make things up as she goes along. We all go along with her.

I start with Christmas. I include her ball gown, us dancing, music notes, and of course, little hot chocolate mugs. Next, I show small signs of the snow day. Snowballs, snowflakes, and snow-coated clothes. Then ever so gently, I use watercolour to paint the river. To emphasise how heavy the rain was, how magical that moment was. *How that was the day, I fell in love.* Finally, I delicately add sparkles to the Eiffel tower and sketch Ambres face, eyes lit up so bright, admiring it intently.

I experiment with so many colours I've lost count, trying different combinations, attempting to get the perfect colour. Whatever will capture this moment best. This piece means a lot to me. It symbolises our journey, Ambre and me. From books to paint brushes to the Eiffel tower and the river. All of it.

I put my earphones in and play some of my inspirational music. Songs that put me in the painting mood, songs that remind me of Ambre. The studio really is the best setting. There are candles in every corner, lighting the room in the best way. Soft, warm light. I have my own painting kit, but anything you need, Viv provides. Since coming here, I've noticed Viv takes on a motherly role with everyone. She's the mother figure to everyone who crosses her path. It's been kind of nice to have a mother figure again. I struggle every day not having my Mam here. So having someone who thinks of me like a son, in a way, it's been really lovely. She goes upstairs into her little apartment and makes food when she knows you haven't eaten; she brings down water every thirty minutes, bugging you until you drink it. She's an angel. It feels like my Mam has sent her to me. What are the chances? I love painting; the closest art studio nearby is owned by Viv. The most motherly woman you'll ever meet. She's also obsessed with animals. Hence the 'pet sanctuary.'

I've finished sketching now, and I'm down to using all the colours I spent forever mixing. I found the perfect shade for everything; I even matched the colour of Ambre's dress perfectly. I feel like everything is perfect for the first time in a while. Ambre and I are good. She *may* even love me the way I love her. We made our dreams come true together. I'm actually *okay*. No more flashbacks, no more worry, because I'm safe. *We're* safe.

I watch Chubbs as he struts out of the 'pet sanctuary' as if he owns the place. He continues through to the other room, and I let him because we let pets roam here for some reason. There's probably food in the other room that he can smell.

I turn my attention back to my painting. It's almost done. The only thing left to paint is the sketch of Ambre and me dancing in the middle of the painting. Colour surrounds that moment. I dip my brush in the perfect shade of blue for Ambre's dress, and suddenly, there's a high pitch, deafening ringing around me. *The fire alarm.* Please, please, please tell me this is a drill.

"FIRE!" Never mind.

I rushedly run over to the next room to help; I guess my degree will come in handy a lot earlier than I imagined. Then, smoke begins to fill the small, enclosed space. Flames climb up the sheer curtain decorating the entire room. It's spreading fast.

"Everyone leave your stuff and head out the front door. Hurry!" I grab the door, keeping it open until everyone is out. "Viv, start calling names from the check-in sheet. Make sure everyone is here. The fire department are on their way. Can somebody tell me how the fire started?" I question urgently.

"Some fat cat knocked a few candles over with its tail." Someone shouts out. That damned cat.

"Okay, first of all, has everyone got their animals?" She asks as if that's the most crucial question.

I search around outside to see if anyone grabbed Chubbs when they ran out; he's not here. He's still in there, I'll be damned if I go home to Ambre without her cat. That cat means the absolute world to her; she trusted me with him. And I won't let her down.

I pass my painting to Viv quickly, and before anyone can object, I swing open the heavy door and rush inside. The door closes behind me with a click. There's no backing out now. *I'm saving that cat.*

I search through the room; I look under tables and behind equipment. No sign. "Chubbs!" I scream to the point my voice cracks. I look around me, but all I can see is black smoke and flames filling the room, clouding my vision. I cough as smoke fills my lungs; I will find this cat even if it kills me.

At least I'd die a hero like my Dad.

The acrid smell of fire surrounds me as I push through. I stumble through an archway and fall into a massive stack of soot-covered books. Several huge shelves surround me, filled top to bottom with books. *Ambre's heaven.* Lay down on a book, filled with evident exhaustion and pain, is Chubbs. Chubbs, who no longer has whiskers, Chubbs, whose ginger fur is now black, and grey. I reach for him, ready to leave this place; he jumps onto the nearest shelf. A shelf which has just caught fire... The weight of Chubbs on the shelf causes it to wobble. It's unstable as it is. Chubbs croaks out a pained noise.

"I know, buddy. I'm sorry." I croak out. I don't recognise the voice that leaves me.

He jumps again onto a higher level of the shelf. It can't handle it. A cold shiver runs down my back as the realisation sets in. That thing is coming down. *Onto me.* I push Chubbs off the ledge to give him a chance of survival. I suddenly jump up, attempting to get away.

The second I move, the shelf creaks and collapses directly onto my leg. Trapping me in the smoke-filled room. Fire continues to climb up the walls, burning everything in sight. The shelf and the thousands of books on it crush my leg fast. My leg starts to go numb. Tingles travel up my leg all the way to my shoulders. I curse out because, damn, that hurts. Pangs of sharp pain stab at my leg continuously, leaving me in agonising pain.

I reach for my leg, trying to pull it out from under the shelf, but my arms don't have the strength. I don't have enough strength left in me to even lift myself. I fall back and hit my head on the hard ground. Aching pain travels around my entire head. I fight to keep my eyes open. I'm not going yet.

Chubbs slowly makes his way to me, looking weak and barely alive, and he collapses by my head. Tears roll down my cheeks uncontrollably. All the air in my lungs is getting filled with smoke. I'm struggling to breathe. I suck in a sharp breath; all I get is smoke. Sweat runs down my head, fire burns into my trapped leg, and everything starts to go numb as the world around me drifts away.

I attempt to move my head to look at Chubbs. I place a shaky, weak arm on his back, trying to let him know he's not alone, I'm still here, and I won't let him never get to see his Ambre again, but he's gone... My heart drops; he's not breathing. "Chubbs," I plead, barely audible. Then everything goes black.

Chapter 24

Ambre

I dropped my class the second the hospital called me as Luc's emergency contact. He's in the hospital. Why the hell is my Luc in the hospital? I'm sitting in the waiting room, sweating like hell because I don't know what's happening. I need answers. What if he's seriously hurt? What could he have possibly done at the art studio? I go on my phone to message Viv and see she's already messaged.

Viv: Hey, Hunny. Though you'd rather hear from me than the news, my building burned down. The fire department are searching for Luc in there now. I'm sure all will be fine, don't you worry.

Searching for Luc? Luc was in there while it burned down? Is Luc alive? My heart pounds uncontrollably in my chest. My breaths get shorter and start coming out faster. Is there enough air in this room? It doesn't feel like it. All of a sudden, I'm sweltering. I attempt to cool myself down with a paper that was in my bag, but it does nothing. My body shakes violently as I stand to search for someone.

"I need a doctor! Somebody, please." I yell out. My voice cracks. Everything around me is overwhelming. People around me are breathing too loud, everyone is too close, I need space, I need Luc, where the hell is my Luc?

A lady in uniform rushes over to me and puts an arm around me. "Hey, you're okay. Sit here, lovely. It's all okay." She says in a soothing voice. Nothing about her is soothing me right now, though. Luc could be dead, and she's telling me everything's okay? Nothing is okay. I can't live without him.

"No, I need Luc. Take me to Luc." I say in hysterics.

"Honey, if you're in the waiting room, it's for a reason. Unfortunately, we can't take you to him right now."

"Is he alive? Please tell me he's alive." I say between sharp breaths. I begin to hyperventilate. I can't breathe. I need information. Why won't anyone give me any damn information?

"I can't answer your questions right now. So hold tight for now, okay? I'll be back."

I fall to the ground and let out a wail. That's a no, isn't it? My Luc, he's gone. No. No. He can't be gone. Shivers roll down my body. I sink to my knees and let the tears pour out of me. I need my Luc back. Everything around me goes blurry; nothing is clear, I can't see. I stumble to my feet and start pushing through doors.

"Madame, you can *not* be back here." Some lady behind a counter shouts.

"I don't care. Take me to Luc, or I'll find him myself." I spit out. She rolls her eyes and points to a door. I rush over to the door in the direction she pointed at. I stagger through the door, and I'm faced with several doctors and nurses.

"Can somebody in this room tell me what the hell is going on with my Luc?" I demand through my tears. This is hell. If I were sent to hell, this would be it. I need Luc; I need him.

"Madame de Roselle? He isn't looking good. I'm so sorry." someone replies apologetically. Blood rushes to my ears as I turn to the door. I lurch through it to find the closest exit. I can't do this. I can't do it.

What is life if not spent with the one you love? I run towards a blurry exit sign.

A hand is placed on my shoulder, and I turn around frantically. "Get off me, please get off me." I plead as I fail to hold composure and fall to the ground. The person from before sits down next to me.

"I'll answer anything you need to know."

243

"What's wrong with my Luc? I need my Luc back." I say more to myself, between heavy breaths that I struggle to get out. "We were told he went back into the building after saving everyone else, turns out he studies fire science. While it was burning down, he got trapped there. I believe he was trying to rescue something. When the fire services found him, he was lying next to a cat who had unfortunately passed away; we think that cat is what he was trying to save. Luc was trapped under a heavy bookshelf, it cut off circulation in his leg, and his lungs were full of smoke. He was barely breathing. We're doing everything in our power to bring him back, Ambre. I promise. And *I'm so so sorry.*"

My heart drops to my stomach. *Chubbs?* Chubbs is gone. Luc is barely alive. Luc risked his life to save Chubbs for me. Luc might die because of me. I should never have asked him to take Chubbs to the studio. This is all my fault. I think I'm going to throw up. *Luc took fire science?* He wanted to surprise me. And I couldn't be prouder of him. I wish he were here for me to tell him.

What if I never get to tell Luc how I feel?

I'm sitting in Luc's room, no longer having a panic attack.

The doctor sat with me for hours. She asked me questions about Luc and me. I told her about all our best memories and how our situation is slightly confusing. But, it made me happy thinking about us. It took my mind off things.

Now I'm sitting in a chair waiting for Luc. I'm trying to process everything. I'm grieving Chubbs, all the while praying I won't have to grieve my best friend. The doctors said they couldn't promise he'll wake up. My heart cracked when they told me. I just have to believe. I'll pray to every God out there. I'll do anything to have my Luc back. One thing I know for sure is that Luc is a fighter. He's been fighting his entire life. He'll continue to fight. If he doesn't do it for himself, he'll do it for me.

Come back to me, Luc.

Vivienne from Luc's art studio walks through the door; why?

"Hey, hunny. I'm sure you want to be alone, but I thought you might want this." She hands me a large canvas.

"Thank you, Viv." I say sincerely as she leaves the room.

I look down at the painting. It's the most beautiful painting I've ever seen. Is that- *it's Luc and me.* It's us dancing in black and white, surrounded by everything that makes us who we are in colour. I turn it over and see the message.

245

'Happy birthday to you, my princess, my girl.'

How long has this taken him? It's incredible. My heart melts as I notice every minor detail he's included. *My boy.* He's always going to be my boy. He's not leaving me.

∧

Hours pass by, and nothing happens. My heart sinks a little more every second Luc doesn't wake up. Nobody is around. It's just Luc and me. I bring my knees to my chest and hug them tight. Then I let myself cry. I let it all go.

"Please come back, Luc. I can't do this without you." I whimper through my tears.

"I'm so completely consumed by you, Luc. You're everywhere I look; you never leave my mind, not even for a second. And I can't survive without you. I'm *helplessly* in love with you. I know that now. *Please* come back so I can tell you that." I cry out as if he can hear me. The absence of Luc, the feeling that I may never see him again, made me realise everything that's been there all along. That life is not worth living if not with him.

"About damn time, princess." A soft, weak voice croaks out.

I immediately rush over to Luc's bed to ensure I'm not going crazy. *My Luc's okay. He's really okay.*

"You're okay? Are you really here? Please tell me my mind isn't playing tricks on me right now." I plead.

"I'm here; this is all real, my love. I'm okay."

I'm now grinning through my tears. I lean down to Luc and kiss him softly. "You're never leaving my side again, Luc." I kiss him again.

"I don't plan on it." He smiles at me.

"I'm deeply in love with you; *you* are my home, Luc. You're my everything. I don't think I would have made it without you. You've broken my heart a million times in the past few hours. Please don't *ever* leave me again."

"I'm in love with you, princess. I always have been and always will be." he runs a hand along my cheek. "You're so incredibly gorgeous." I laugh light-heartedly through the tears that won't stop.

"You're incredibly handsome. And maybe I was drooling at the river." I laugh.

"I knew it." He states and pulls me to lie with him.

"I love you, Luc. Forever and always."

"I love you, Ambre. For infinity."

⚶ Epilogue ⚶

Three years later

Luc

"I love the stars. Don't you love the stars?" Ambre questions as we lay on a blanket by the Eiffel tower.

I'm not watching the stars; I'm watching her. My girlfriend. My world. My future wife. "I do love the stars." Translating to I love *you.*

"Do you remember when we did this *three* years ago?" She questions excitedly.

"I do. It's the day I fell in love with you, princess." She turns to her side to face me and smiles.

"I knew I loved you. But my love was completely unwanted at first. I didn't want to love you. I thought it'd ruin everything; I was scared. But it didn't. It made it better. I've never been happier to be wrong."

"I didn't intend to fall in love with my best friend either. But I don't regret a thing, princess." I place a soft kiss on her forehead.

"I can't *believe* I ever doubted us. We were always inevitable."

"And I knew it from the start; see, I'm the smart one here."

"Oh hush, my smartness was just faltering." She giggles as she cuddles up to my arm.

"Sure it was, princess." I kiss her deeply as the stars shine above us.

"Luc, I've got something to tell you."

Panic rises inside me for a second. Is this going to be good or bad? "Hit me."

"My book became a *New York Times* best-seller today." She grins at me.

My mouth drops, "Oh my, God. That's incredible, Ambre. I'm so proud of you." My girl did it. She'd been writing *Unwanted love* for over a year. She never believed in herself. But she's gone and done it. That's my girl.

It's 00:58. I pull Ambre to stand with me. "Ugh, why are we standing. I want to lie down." She whines. She won't be whining in a second; I hope not, anyway.

I hold both of her hands in mine, "Ambre de Roselle, you are the craziest person I've ever met. There isn't a soul in this world who could ever compare to you. You light up every room you walk into. You sit in the corner of a crowded room reading a book and still shine brighter than everyone combined. You're truly incredible. I've known it since the day you said yes to being my best friend. We've spent our entire lives together as best friends; now I want to spend the rest of it with you as my wife." I get down on one knee as the clock hits one am. And the Eiffel tower sparkles beside us. "Ambre, will you marry me?"

She suddenly drops to her knees with me, and tears start building up in her eyes. Ambre puts her hand out to me and nods frantically.

"Yes, yes, yes. I want nothing more than to be your wife, Luc. I love you, I love you, I love you." She says and jumps into my arms before kissing me urgently.

"Hold on, hold on," I laugh, "Ring." Ambre smiles giddily and puts her hand out again. I slowly slide the lilac heart-cut diamond onto her ring finger.

"We're getting married!" Ambre exclaims and jumps into my arms once again.

"We are indeed, princess."

"Since I'm your princess and we're getting married, that makes you my prince."

"It sure does. I think moving to the *city of love* with my best friend is the best decision I've ever made."

"My best friend became the love of my life. It was *definitely* the best decision I've ever made." Ambre agrees.

I smile against her mouth and pull her into a tight embrace. *My fiancé. My forever.*

The end

Acknowledgements

What a journey this has been. Unwanted Love is the first novel I've ever written, it may be short but it owns my heart, and gosh it was a rollercoaster, to say the least. And I adored every second. My dream has always been to be an author, writing this book I have made my dream come true. And it's all thanks to the people around me who gave me their honesty, love and support the entire time.

Ambre and Luc have been my comfort characters for the past year. I've been able to find safety and comfort in them. I know they're the type of people I'd want at my side. I'm going to miss them. I hope you fall in love with Ambre and Luc the same way I did.

I want to say a huge thank you to Eliana. My favourite French friend. Without Eliana's help with certain French phrases, I would have been lost. I love and adore you so much, Eliana. I can't wait to one day meet you, and spend our time exploring Paris together.

My uncles amazing girlfriend, Chelsea. Chelsea, without your help this book wouldn't be how it is today. Your notes, and your advice mean more than you'll ever know. Thank you for taking your time to read and annotate my first book, you helped me live my dream.

P.s, if I make it as an author, you're automatically hired ;)

My Mum has been my greatest supporter. From hand-writing her short stories since six years old to writing this novel. She has kept and read every little book I made her. She's my number one fan. I couldn't have done this without her support and positivity. As she always says, you have to manifest the things you want. I manifested becoming an author. And I made that happen. Thank you Mum. I love you most.

My friends and family have been a huge part of this. They examined my many covers. They read several blurbs. They helped me throughout this whole process. They gave me love and support, reminding me I can do this, I can do anything I set my mind to, and I can make my dreams come true. I threw in a few inside jokes, and dedications to them throughout Unwanted Love. Let's see if they can find them.

And finally, I need to say the biggest thank you to you. Whoever is reading this right now. Just by reading this, you're making my dreams come true. I truly hope you loved reading this book as much as I enjoyed writing it.

Until next time....

Keep a look out for...

Unwanted Lies - Unwanted series 2

Unwanted Hate - Unwanted series 3

Printed in Great Britain
by Amazon

13161057R00149